THE GOVERNESS

ELIZABETH JOHNS

The Governess

PROLOGUE

Bath, England 1814

ADELAIDE STOOD in the entrance hall of Miss Bell's Finishing School for Young Ladies, feeling a similar trepidation as she had four years ago when she had first set foot inside. Then, she had worried about being accepted as an orphaned poor relation who had been sent to school to be out of the way. Now, her friends were off to partake in the London Season and she was to take her first post as a governess.

She pulled on her faded blue merino pelisse and turned slowly in the round, domed room, trying to take in everything about this place that had come to feel like home. Inhaling the scent of the lilies which sat in a vase near the door, she took her bonnet down from its hook.

"Where are you going?"

Adelaide turned towards the voice of Caroline, one of her four closest friends and room-mates.

"I thought to take one more walk," she answered softly, trying to hide the emotion building inside her as she tied the ribbons of her old poke bonnet under her chin.

"Alone?" Caroline questioned.

Adelaide lifted one shoulder. "It no longer matters. Tomorrow my reputation will be of little consequence."

"Why will you not accept my sponsor's offer and come to London with me?" Caroline took Adelaide's hand as she pleaded.

"Caro, we have discussed this. It is a most gracious offer, but I see no point in prolonging the inevitable. I would—could—be nothing more than your shadow."

"You would not!" she protested. "There is a gentleman out there who will care nothing for your reduced circumstances."

"You are a dear for saying so, but you know I speak the truth." Adelaide shook her head as footsteps sounded on the stairs.

"What is going on?" Jo asked as she and Penelope joined them in the entrance hall.

"Adelaide is going for a walk alone," Caroline announced with disapproval.

"No she is not. We will all go," Jo said decisively.

"Are you still trying to convince her to go to London?" Penelope asked.

Adelaide sighed. This conversation had been repeated every day for the past month, since she had announced she had taken a position in Yorkshire. She waited while her friends donned their cloaks and bonnets and they walked out onto Great Pulteney Street. Automatically, they headed along the street towards Sydney Gardens, where, for the past four years, they had walked every day it had not rained.

"I think it is time we accept the inevitable, girls."

"Perhaps your employer will be handsome and want to marry you," Penelope said in her typically pragmatic way.

"Do not be ridiculous, Pen. He no doubt has a wife who would object."

"It could happen." She defended her suggestion as the other girls shook their heads.

"I will keep an eye out for a rich gentleman who will care not if you have no dowry," Jo said practically.

"And I will try to find a husband who has a home in Yorkshire," Caro insisted earnestly.

"I cannot think of a husband." Adelaide interrupted their fantasies as they reached their favourite spot within the labyrinth. She stopped and turned to face her dearest friends. "And if I did happen to receive an offer, I could not marry for mercenary reasons."

"You would rather be a governess?" Caroline asked with astonishment.

"I am no Charlotte Lucas." All the girls shuddered at the thought of the hideous Mr. Collins from *Pride and Prejudice*, one of the books they had read over and over together through their years at school. "It is universally acknowledged amongst us that anything is better than marrying out of desperation."

"Of course it is!" they insisted.

"Yet Mr. Darcy is fictional."

"Adelaide!" Caro exclaimed as though she had spoken heresy.

"I do not begrudge you for going to London," Adelaide continued. "I am mostly sad because everything will change. You will all marry and move to various parts of England."

Caroline burst into tears as Adelaide struggled to contain her own desire to sob uncontrollably. It felt as though everyone else was moving on with their futures and she would be stuck in a never-ending cycle of being an upstairs servant.

"This was not supposed to happen, Addy," Jo said, dabbing her nose with a handkerchief.

"We were all supposed to go to London together and marry for love!" Caroline insisted.

Jo nudged Caroline with her elbow. "Those were silly promises we made to each other when we were children."

"I want you to keep those promises...for me. There is no reason you should all suffer."

"It does not seem fair," Caroline protested.

"If I know you have found happiness, it will make my circumstances more bearable. Then I may come to be governess to your children," she added dryly.

"Oh, Addy!" Caro exclaimed. "You must not say such things!"

"Whyever not? I am counting on it. Now, let us not be sad. It is the last night we will all be together."

"For now," Jo corrected, though Adelaide knew better than to hope.

CHAPTER 1

*A*delaide vowed she would not cry over what she could not change, so she tried not to think of what she was leaving behind as the horses' hooves clopped against the stones. Waving a last farewell to her friends from the school, she settled in to the plush blue velvet squabs, feeling strangely alone. It would be several long days in the carriage, peaceful time she would cherish.

"Probably the last hours of peace I shall ever have," she mused as she watched the town of Bath and its familiar golden stone pass by until the buildings faded into hedges and countryside. Spring was finally emerging, trees were budding, and daffodils and wild flowers could be seen in patches dotting the meadows as they drove by.

Once the scenery became monotonous, she pulled out Edgeworth's *Belinda* to pass the hours, but felt nauseous from trying to read while moving. A book on courtship and marriage was hardly appealing to one whom was walking away from any such opportunity in the future. As though she had a choice, she reflected with a sigh. Could she have made a match, had she gone with Caroline to London? Doubts assailed her as the carriage took her farther away from Bath. Laying the book aside, she was determined to be positive about her future life, even though realism would not cease.

"I shall not be a crotchety old governess," she vowed. "There will be joy in my life and that of my charges."

In reality, she knew very little about her employers. She had given her requirements to the agency and they had found her this post. For one, they were being most generous towards her. She had expected to travel by the stage, and yet, they had sent their own carriage for her. It had been some time since she had been in a carriage, and never one this well appointed, not even her aunt Hogg's.

Several images of what her future home would be like had played through her mind—much though she tried to avoid predisposing her judgements upon people she had never met. Even she had to admit to herself that she was fearful of a disgusting old pig of a master who would try to take advantage of her lowered status. One did not live amongst silly young girls without hearing rumours of every sort.

Most would dream of a handsome young duke who happened to be pining away at his country house until his beautiful governess arrived to show him the error of his single ways.

Laughing aloud at the idiocy of the idea, she muttered to herself, "Clearly he will be neither young nor single since he has children. Well, I suppose he could be a widower and his wife died very young. No, they would have a nurse not a governess, so that is not a possibility."

"The most likely situation is an average country house, with a insipidly normal husband and wife, with plain, boring children. Therefore, I am destined to have a very plain life...but a joyful one," she reminded herself with every bit of the sarcasm she felt. She could only pray that the man and woman would be congenial and leave her to her own devices.

"Start as you mean to go on," Miss Bell had advised. Unfortunately for that maxim, she was crossing into an unknown divide from which she could not return.

"Enough of that," she chided, and again determined to think of something else. Besides her future and thinking of what her friends were going to be doing in London without her, her thoughts could only go straight to her brother, away on the Peninsula fighting Napoleon. Having written her new direction to him, she could only hope that he received some of her letters. Faithfully, she wrote to him each week but she had yet to receive a letter from him that year. There had been no news of his death and she refused to give up hope. It had been so long since she had seen Philip—not since their parent's deaths, in fact. He had been little more than a boy when he left to join the army, and she had been sent to Miss Bell's school. What would Philip be like when he returned? If only she knew he was unharmed! She shook her head. There was no safe place for her thoughts at the moment. It was going to be a very long, lonely week in the carriage, despite travelling with every comfort.

When the carriage at last pulled through the gates of her new residence—she could not bring herself to think of it as home—she was relieved by the beauty surrounding her. She watched out of the window, waiting for her first glimpse of the house. They climbed up and down through some green, pasture-covered hills, then through a wooded park, so it was half an hour before the house came into view. The grounds were extensive, indicating great wealth on the part of her new patrons. Having been in a boarding house in Bath, she longed to explore every inch of this estate.

"Please let my charges not be lazy sloths," she prayed. "Well, if they are, we will have to change that. It should be simple enough," she said decidedly. If she did not find herself free of this conveyance soon, she knew she would lose her mind. Every inch of her ached to move about and she was uncertain whether or not her joints would be locked in place.

At last, the house came into sight. It was a large Elizabethan manor, its orange brick bright with the sun's afternoon rays upon it. It was almost eerie, but she refused to be intimidated. Fanciful towers seemed to watch their approach. The outline of the roof was elaborate, decorating a large, square house with matching oriel windows flanking either side of the entrance.

No one greeted them as the carriage pulled to a halt in front of the grand edifice. She wondered if they might be expecting her at the servant's entrance. No, her circumstances might be reduced, but she was still a lady. *Start as you mean to go on.* The footman opened the door for her and she gratefully alighted and tried not to stretch her limbs ungracefully. She did stretch her neck heavenward, and took note of her surroundings, but no one else appeared. It was too quiet.

Walking forward with a sense of impending doom, her footsteps crunched loudly on the gravel in the silent forecourt. She dropped the knocker on the massive wooden door. There was no answer, so she rapped again with a bit more force. A few minutes passed, and by this time, the footman and driver were standing immobile, watching her.

Adelaide turned to face them. "Are you quite certain we are at the right place?"

"Yes, miss. This is my master's country estate," the driver reassured her.

"Should we try the servant's entrance?"

"I suppose no harm could come from it," the driver said, though the footman looked wary. Adelaide refused to climb back into the landau, and chose the footpath around the house. When they arrived and climbed the steps to the door, it was open but there was no one inside.

There was a delicious-smelling soup in a kettle over a fire, and Adelaide stopped fretting. "Someone shall turn up soon. They would not have left a fire going if they had abandoned the house," she pronounced.

"True enough, miss. We will bring your trunks in and Mrs. Allen should be able to tell us which room is yours."

"Very good. Where is she to be found?"

Someone must have seen them arrive, for at that moment a groom burst into the kitchen, announcing breathlessly, "Master Freddy and Master Harry have gone missing! They were nowhere to be found in the house, so everyone has set out scouring the grounds trying ter find them afore nightfall. The moors are a dangerous place to be in the daylight and if they fall into the quicksand..." He let his words trail off. Even Adelaide had heard of how dangerous the moors could be.

"Can I help?" she asked, unsure of what to do next.

"No, miss. I think you should stay here in case the boys return. They are always kicking up a lark, and this may be their idea of one. Nurse is too old to be chasing after two unruly lads."

Boys? Yes, she supposed he had said Master Freddy and Master Harry. Why in Heaven's name was she here? Boys needed tutors, not governesses. Adelaide sighed deeply. This would not be a suitable post for her after all.

Untying her bonnet and pelisse, she began to wander through the halls of the house. It was well cared for with modern furnishings, yet it felt hollow and uninviting—much like her aunt's house had felt.

She walked through the great hall, the heels of her sturdy, practical half-boots echoing with each step on the parquet floor. There were two large fireplaces, one at either end, and giant animal heads flanked the adjacent walls which were lined with spears and swords. It felt medieval. Not wanting to stay in a room where she was being watched, she moved on to a door and peeked inside to discover the dining room. Her stomach gave a small rumble, reminding her that she had not yet had her supper, but she was not inclined to help herself from the larder either. She could envision the sight—plum jelly dripping down her chin as all the residents of Harlton Park returned. What an introduction that would be! She giggled a little nervously as she closed the door to the dining room and went on to the next.

A whiff of leather and books greeted her as she entered the library and, even though the room seemed as large as Miss Bell's school, this was the most likely place for her to feel comfortable. She knew where she would take her respite if she ever found any—and were she permitted. There had to be thousands of books lining each wall. She fingered the spines lovingly as she made her way around the room, staring upwards at a balcony which contained even more leather-bound volumes.

It was here she found a small door, probably for the servants, yet she could not help but investigate. Immediately, her nose was met by the scents of tobacco and musk. *This must be the master's domain*, she thought. Adelaide knew she should turn and walk back out, but it was the first sign of inhabitance and she felt drawn to know more about who owned this unwelcoming fortress.

It was a masculine room, she could see, though the light was beginning to fade. It was cosy with dark mahogany panelling, an imposing wooden desk, and some comfortable chairs flanking the fireplace. Her gaze went past a portrait over the mantel and immediately was drawn back.

"Is this the master?" she questioned aloud as she stared. There was a presence about this man she could not quite explain. Her heart began to speed up as though she had never seen a handsome man before. Perhaps the artist had taken liberties, but even so she did not think the subject could be ugly. Tawny hazel eyes stared down at her from a face possessed of a fine jaw and framed with honey locks. The longer she stared the more his eyes seemed to cast an arrogant, knowing look at her. Her gaze swept downward, knowing the figure would be equally fine to match the face. He wore riding dress with Hessian boots displaying an elegant, yet athletic form. A beautiful bay horse stood to his side—a perfect specimen to match his master.

Adelaide was startled by a noise and her heart thumped inside her chest as though she had been caught trespassing like a naughty schoolgirl. She hurried from the room and out into the entrance hall, where an angry servant was holding two young, mud-drenched urchins up by their collars. Soon, what Adelaide surmised were the rest of the household servants came pouring in behind. Adelaide at once shut her jaw, which she was certain was gaping.

These were her charges?

"You must be Miss Elliot. Welcome to Harlton Park. I hereby give notice." An older woman, whom Adelaide assumed to be the nurse-maid, stamped away, muttering under her breath.

ROBERT CLOSED his book with contentment, then expelled a deep sigh —one that was filled with a host of emotions he had yet to express even to himself. He was a confirmed bachelor, and had no intention, nor inclination, towards the paternal. No, having children was something he did not think about and tended to avoid at all costs.

Now, in nature's way of irony, he had acquired two wards. It was not that he regretted taking care of his friend's children, for he had nothing but fond and honourable thoughts for his fellow officer in arms. Colonel Appleton would have done the same for him. It was more that he questioned why he, of all people, had been chosen for the task. No doubt Appleton had hoped the unthinkable would not happen to him. Robert paused. It should have been he who had fallen...he with no children, no ties, no fatherly instinct...

So he did what any good guardian would do—he installed them at his country estate and hired a governess for them. It was not that Robert was without feeling, but he truly believed the children were better off with guidance from a governess rather than the inept direction of one who knew nothing of children. Having satisfied his sense of duty, he arrested further thoughts of his wards, knowing that should a need arise, the governess, steward or solicitor would know where to find him.

He happily returned his thoughts to his bachelor ways of doing exactly what he wanted when it suited him, much in the footsteps of his scandalous ancestor, Beau Fielding. Well aware he was quite fortunate, he had watched many of his friends fall into the trap of matrimony and become as puppets led around by a string. He shuddered while mentally patting himself on the back for having continued to elude the matchmaking mamas of the *ton*. Even though untitled, he was from one of the oldest, and wealthiest families in Society. The Fieldings had a knack for investing and had been able to maintain their estates in comfort for generations. Robert was not uncharitable; he was quite happy to share his wealth with any number of worthy causes. He even chose a female for his wards rather than a tutor, allowing them some maternal affection before they were sent away to

Harrow. Afterwards, when they could speak intelligently, he fully intended to take them in hand and teach them the ways of Society.

Draining the last drop of brandy from his glass, he set it down on the table, and stood to check his neckcloth in the looking-glass. A full evening lay ahead after his fencing match with his army friends, he was to dine at his club and then meet Mrs. Vanover, a merry widow, for the theatre.

Satisfied with his plans, he went to the entrance hall to fetch his hat and gloves, whereupon his butler, Percy, handed him a letter. He raised his eyebrows at the outstretched hand containing the offensive object, which his instinct told him he should leave until the morrow.

"It is from Harlton Park, sir."

"Place it on my desk and I will attend to it in the morning." Robert used the term *morning* loosely for he rarely greeted the day before noon.

"It came by post, sir."

Robert stared at the letter a few moments longer before reluctantly holding out his hand. He returned to the library with a heavy sigh, knowing there was nothing on these pages he wanted to see.

R. Fielding Esq.,
   Sir,

I BEG LEAVE to inform you, in case you have not already been notified, the boys' nurse quit her position upon my arrival. It would seem the boys are in need of more care than a governess can provide. Please consider visiting to advise and assume a closer hand in their upbringing.

I BEG TO REMAIN, Sir,
   Your obedient servant,

. . .

Miss A. Elliot

DEEPLY ANNOYED, he thrust back his coat-tails and sat on the edge of his chair at his great mahogany desk. He whipped a piece of paper out of a drawer and dipped his quill in the standish.

Miss A. Elliot,
  Madam,

If you are incapable of managing two young boys, I will ask my solicitor to find a replacement.

Your obedient servant,
  —Fielding

HE SANDED THEN FOLDED the letter and sealed it. Who precisely did this woman think she was? Mr. Winton, his secretary, had assured him she came with impeccable references from a select school for ladies. Perhaps they should have chosen someone more seasoned, but Nurse had asked for someone younger—more energetic had been her precise words—to be able to keep up with two lively boys.

Perhaps they would be better suited to school, where they could be with other children their age and learn discipline. He would have Winton look into it.

Not wanting this to spoil his evening, he poured himself another brandy to calm his irritation. Taking a sip, he thumped his fist down on his desk with deliberate calmness. Who was this upstart of a governess to tell him how to manage his charges? And why the devil had he, of all people, been left two children to bring up?

He ran his hand through his hair, which he knew very well only dishevelled it in a way that added to his allure. Dealing with women could be a nuisance, but it could also be wonderful when they knew their place. He smiled to himself and tipped back the remains of his glass. He set it down and inhaled deeply before sallying forth yet again to begin his evening. He would not think of the children again that night—nor their despot of a governess. If she complained again he would dismiss her and that was his last thought of her for the night.

CHAPTER 2

*A*delaide balled up the curt note from her employer and growled in frustration. *What a pompous...*her thoughts trailed off before she said something unladylike. He clearly had no care for these children, as he had not even bothered to come to greet them, according to Mrs. Allen, the housekeeper. No wonder they were misbehaving; they had no one who cared for them. They needed a parental figure and Adelaide could only do so much. These boys were a handful—to say the least—and she needed some help. She could not let them out of her sight or they would be off on a spree, as her brother would have phrased it. They were fairly well behaved when she was giving them her full attention, but Heaven forbid she go to the necessary, or she would find them escaped.

Besides their escapade into the moor and the quicksand, they had plucked feathers from Mrs. Coddle's rooster, they had rolled in the mud with Mr. Jones's pigs and they had taken one of the master's stallions out for a ride. It was a wonder they had not broken one of their necks yet. All of this they had achieved in less than three weeks' time.

"Where could they be this time?" she wondered aloud as she searched the grounds. She was aware of their start, so they could not have gone too far. Next time she needed to relieve herself, she would tie them to a post! Telling herself she must think like a little boy, she headed away from the house.

"Here birdie, birdie!" She finally heard a voice call followed by a loud plop.

Oh, dear. It sounded like they were in the trees. Picking up her faded grey skirts, she hastened through the kitchen garden and the wicket gate into the orchard.

"Look out, below!" she heard one of them bellow. She barely had time to look up and see a plum shoot by her head.

"Master Freddy and Master Harry, come down this minute!" She used her stern voice which she had had to adopt very quickly in the past week.

"You ain't going to birch us are you?" The head groom had birched them soundly for running away with the stallion.

"You are not," she corrected. "Come down here, now."

The two red-headed, freckled-faced boys slowly climbed down from the trees, hanging their heads in well-rehearsed repentance. That was part of the difficulty—she had a hard time punishing them when they gazed at her with those forlorn eyes. It was as though they could not help themselves with regards to their behaviours. They needed more activity than one person alone could provide.

"What do you have to say for yourselves, boys?" Adelaide crossed her arms over her chest and looked down her nose as her old governess had done.

"We are right sorry, miss. It was just a lark. We didn't mean no harm."

"Have you not learned, after every episode thus, that you cannot run away as you please?"

Freddy hung his head. "Yes, miss, but we didn't go to any of the tenant farms this time."

"A minor improvement, I grant you...however, only just."

"What are you going to do to us this time?" young Harry asked.

She tapped her finger against her chin as if thinking hard. "What do you think would be suitable?"

Freddy and Harry eyed each other with obvious discomfort.

Freddy shrugged. "Writing our numbers or declensions fifty times each?"

"I think we have done that enough for one week. Come with me, I have a better idea."

Adelaide left them at the stables with the head groom, to muck out some stalls. It seemed manual labour was a more reasonable punishment and would perhaps tire them—at least she hoped. The boys would be occupied for some time, so she opened the door to the kitchen and dropped wearily into a seat at the table, across from where Cook was mixing some ingredients.

Cook clucked her tongue. "Where were the rascals this time?"

"In the orchard, launching plums at the poor birds."

"Boys get up to mischief—the master certainly did—but they need a firm hand. I don't know what he expects a lady governess to do with them. These two ain't going to be gracing any ball rooms at the rate they're going."

Adelaide was inclined to agree. They would be lucky to see another year of life at this rate.

This was the most that Cook, or any of the servants for that matter, had spoken to her directly. She wanted to know more about the master, but she had been afraid to ask. It was a lonely world, being a governess. Not quite one of the family and not quite a servant.

"Does the master visit often?"

"Whenever it suits him, I suppose. He comes twice a year, regular-like, and drops in whenever it takes his fancy. At least, he did afore he went to war. I'd say it's not like him not to come and see to his responsibilities, though."

"Perhaps he will when he receives my letter."

Cook paused in her stirring and eyed Adelaide...perhaps with suspicion, but perhaps with a hint of respect.

"Mayhap," was all she said.

It was a few hours later when the groom brought two sodden boys back to her. She looked at them and was afraid to ask.

"I took the liberty of washing them off in the horse trough, miss. I expect they will sleep well for you tonight."

Adelaide nodded. "Thank you, Jeb."

The boys ate their meagre dinner of mutton and turnips, and did not complain when they did not receive a pudding. They went to bed without any fuss and Adelaide vowed to start the next day with activity. After an exhausting day, she went to her room near the nursery. It was more luxurious than her room at Miss Bell's, which she had shared, but simple by the nobility's standards. There was a bed, a small desk, a washing-stand and a chair. The paper on the walls was pale green with cream stripes, while matching green curtains framed the small window. The view from the window looked out over the thickly wooded park, and a partial view of the lake. It would do, but she could not help missing her friends and wondering how different her life would be if her parents were still alive.

"What the devil?" Robert asked when he entered the parlour to be faced with two urchins and a bedraggled girl, who all looked as though they had been cleaning chimneys.

Three pairs of blue eyes looked up at him from beneath the soot but only one flashed fire, and suddenly his interest was stirred.

"I assume you are Mr. Fielding?"

"You have the advantage of me. Whom do I have the pleasure of addressing?" he asked dryly, though he suspected he knew.

"I am Miss Elliot and these are your wards, Masters Freddy and Harry Appleton. They decided it would be a lark to stuff every chimney at Harlton Park with pillows. When we left, the fire had been put out, but the western wing was uninhabitable from smoke. We have travelled to London without stopping, save for changing horses, since these terrors could not be trusted to behave."

Robert considered the disarray before him. He was trying to assimilate the fact that his country estate had caught on fire, while this petite dragon was the governess he had hired and he had two wards he was going to have to deal with quickly. "I assume no one was injured?"

"No, thank God."

Remaining silent as he thought, he moved forward and looked down his nose at the boys, from head to dirty boot. An intimidating stare always worked with new recruits in the field. He circled them twice before speaking.

"What do you have to say for yourselves?"

"S-s-sorry, sir."

"You owe Miss Elliot an apology."

"We are sorry, miss. We didn't mean nothing by it. We just wanted to see if we could catch some birds."

He met this answer with a disgusted sniff.

"And how do you propose to make up for damaging my estate?" Robert asked.

Both boys seem to shrink backwards. Warily, they glanced at each other.

He clasped his hands behind his back and resumed circling around the two boys who remained standing at attention. After an appropriate time to terrify them sufficiently, he eventually spoke.

"By my estimation, even if I used your inheritance and your manual labour for the rest of your lives, you would not be able to pay for the damages."

The older boy gulped.

"Did you behave this way when your father was alive?"

"N-n-no, sir."

"Do you think he would be proud of your behaviour?"

"N-n-no, sir."

"Then I shall give you one more opportunity. If you so much as do one thing without permission from Miss Elliot or myself, you will be sent to the workhouse. Do you understand me?"

"Yes, sir."

"If, and only if, there are no more antics, you will be allowed a walk through the park this afternoon. Do I have your word as gentleman that there will be no further mischief?"

"Yes, sir."

He opened the door to the entrance hall. "Please take these boys," he said to the butler, "and have them bathed. Then please send Mr. Winton to see that they are properly clothed." The boys went without arguing. "Guard them. Do not let them out of your sight."

Robert turned back to face the governess and with his quizzing glass looked at her more thoroughly. He could tell it irritated her by the way she tapped her foot and her chin jutted upwards. He resisted the urge to chuckle.

"Well, if you have nothing to say, I will be on my way," she snapped.

This impertinent, filthy creature meant to leave these beings here and leave? No, she would not be allowed to deposit them like stray kittens and run away.

"No."

In hindsight, it was not the most intelligent thing to say, but he was used to having his wishes obeyed without explanation.

"I beg your pardon?"

"Wait. Please." He could see her jaw was clenched but she did stop. He closed the door and he turned back to Miss…Elliot, was it?

"Did you receive my note?" she asked sharply.

"I received your demands. And did you receive my reply?"

"Do you refer to your insults?" she asked, icy disdain freezing her tone.

Robert inclined his head. "Take it as you wish." He could see it took great effort for her not to lash out at him. He had little doubt she would enjoy planting him a facer, tiny though she was.

He wanted to know why she had thought it was acceptable to bring the boys here, but he could see by her state it was no time to ask such a question. She was ready to leave and some thing, most likely insanity, was telling him to try to make her stay.

"Whatever you have to say, please do so. I refuse to accept the blame for their behaviour. When I arrived, they had run off to trap themselves in quicksand. Whenever I needed a moment to…myself—" She blushed adorably."—they would run away to one of the tenant farms to amuse themselves in the pigsty or steal one of your stallions and race it across the park. These boys need more than one young woman can give them. They need an army." She mumbled the last.

Robert admitted to himself that he had not realized they were so wild, but he would never admit as much to this young, opinionated woman, whom he suspected was a beauty beneath the dirt.

"So you mean to leave them here and run away?" he asked calmly.

Her eyes flashed sparks at him again. He thought he had appealed to her honour and that perhaps, by challenging her, he might be able to convince her to stay.

"Oh yes, indeed," she surprised him by saying.

"And where were you intending to go?"

"Where I should have gone in the first place—to accept the hospitality of my friends."

Robert felt his brow wrinkle. He did not wish to be left alone with these unknown little beings. "Why did you not do so in the first place?"

"Pride," she whispered. Backing, she turned and began to walk towards the door.

"And it does not bruise your pride to walk away from a commitment?" he asked acidly.

"Pride is overrated," she told the door.

"Will you not stay until I find a suitable replacement?"

"Such a person does not exist. What they need is someone to be a father to them." She turned and looked at him pointedly.

"I see I am to be judged and hanged without a trial. Very well." She had the grace to look away. He would dearly love to know if she was blushing beneath the soot. "I must go out, so if you desire to bathe and change your clothing, I will then take you where you wish to go."

CHAPTER 3

*A*delaide followed the housekeeper up a beautiful wooden staircase. Passing through a plushly carpeted hallway lined with paintings of hunting scenes, they came to a spare room opulently decorated in deep greens and puce. It all felt very masculine—as was its master. The painting at Harlton Park had captured him well, except for the way he stole the air from a room with his presence, She was grateful he was allowing her to wash. In truth, she had no idea where to find her friends in this big city. It was a short reprieve from her impending poverty.

Where was Mrs. Fielding? No doubt, in the manner of ladies, she was out making calls or shopping—or avoiding her maddening husband. Adelaide had not expected him to be so handsome. After his treatment of her, she had expected an ogre with a double chin and sweating pate. Instead, she had been met with an imposing man dressed in the height of fashion, with nary a stitch out of place and boots so shiny she could see her reflection in them. His hair was honey-coloured and his eyes were a light hazel. Almost perpetually hooded, they appeared bored, and yet, she was certain they missed nothing.

"I'll have a bath sent up for you, miss," the housekeeper said.

Adelaide barely registered the words, she was so distracted by her thoughts of the master.

"May I perhaps borrow an old gown from Mrs. Fielding?" Adelaide asked, feeling somewhat shy.

The housekeeper narrowed her gaze. "There is no Mrs. Fielding. You have nothing else?"

"I will have to make shift, in that case. We had no time to gather our belongings. Our only thought was to escape the fire."

"I will see what I can do with your dress. We have no young maids, since this is a bachelor establishment, and I am afraid you would be lost in one of my dresses."

"Thank you. Then I may be on my way." Somehow she needed to justify her honourableness to this woman, who nodded approvingly at her statement.

Several servants appeared with a tub and filled it with warm water. She noticed their sideways glances as they tried not to gawk at her state. There would be gossip aplenty below stairs this day.

When they had finished the task and left, Adelaide stepped behind a screen and handed her filthy gown to the housekeeper, who clucked her tongue at it.

Why had the scoundrel not mentioned he was a bachelor, nor yet any of the servants at Harlton Park? She bit her lower lip.

"Because he thinks of you as a servant and nothing more," she muttered to herself.

In fairness, despite her genteel birth, it was now all she was fit for. When she thought of the one gown, the very little money she had to her name, and losing this position...but she was not about to beg to stay here with two hell-born imps and a self-important dandy.

Sinking deep into the steaming, lavender-scented water in the large tub, she decided she could almost forgive him for some of his dandyism. This was as close to heaven on earth as she might ever get again.

For the first time, she was forced to consider her options. While the thought of losing her position so quickly and having nowhere else to go had crossed her mind, she knew she would have a temporary haven with her schoolfellows. She had very little money at her disposal, however, and would probably have to forfeit the week's wages she had earned. A new dress would be beyond her reach either way. Sighing, she wondered if she could perhaps beg a cast-off gown from each of her friends. This might be a sign that being a governess was not her calling...mayhap one of her friends knew of someone who needed a companion? There was nothing to be gained by fretting, she told herself fiercely. Mr. Fielding had offered to take her to her friends—she certainly could not stay here alone with him, even if he did think her a servant. The impropriety of such behaviour had been ingrained in her from an early age. Yet, a little voice in the back of her mind questioned, would she consider propriety so important if she was on the streets and starving?

When the housekeeper knocked on the door an hour later, Adelaide reluctantly began to pull her pruned body from the tub. Her gown and pelisse almost looked blue again.

"Thank you for brushing my clothes."

"I am sorry I couldn't help you more. Here, I'll help with your hair." The housekeeper took a pitcher and rinsed the soap from her hair. A maid was a luxury she had not had since before her parents died.

She climbed from the tub and dried herself before putting her clothing back on. Everything reeked of smoke. Slowly, she picked the tangles out of her hair then wound her thick waves into a loose chignon. There was no time to allow it to dry. A few curls escaped around her temple, but she knew there was nothing to be done about them in the damp air. Unruly hair and the stink of her apparel were the least of her worries.

As she gathered her few possessions back into her small reticule, she decided to wish the boys well. They were not ill-mannered children, they just had more energy and curiosity than was good for them. She climbed the staircase to an upper floor, where she assumed there was a nursery. Hearing their voices, she opened the door. They were standing, clean, near the window, looking out at the city and the roof tops with their smoking chimneys.

"I came to take my leave of you."

"You are leaving us here already?" little Harry asked sadly.

"Yes, I am afraid so," she replied as she gently combed back a stray lock of his hair with her hand.

"Is it because of us?" Freddy asked. "We did not mean to get you sent away."

"You're a great gun!" Harry echoed his innocent sentiments.

"I know you did not mean anything by it, but this is for the best. Mr. Fielding will take good care of you."

"Do you really think he will send us to the workhouse?"

"If you keep burning his houses down, there will be no other choice," she said as sternly as she could, hoping they would understand the gravity of their capers.

"We will do better, we promise, Miss Elliot. Will you stay, please? You are the only one who has been nice to us since Papa died."

"Mr. Fielding will surely send you to school soon. You will be much happier there with other boys your age."

She gave each of the boys a swift hug and made her way back downstairs. Even though she was tempted, she would not leave Mr. Fielding waiting any longer.

ROBERT DID NOT THINK EVEN the Queen would be so long at her bath. He had sent the housekeeper to prompt Miss Elliot after an hour. However, even after finishing her toilette, the dratted female went upstairs! He could not help but sneak up behind her to see what the impertinent chit was up to.

At first, he had been half tempted to send her on her way without offering a bath, but he had been too curious about her, and she was his employee, after all. No employee of his had ever been dismissed and put out in the cold. In actuality, of course, he had not let her go, she had made the pronouncement to leave, which, perversely, made him want to know more about her. She certainly did not seem to be someone well fitted for service. Then, as he had stood outside the nursery about to scold her, he had heard her talking with the boys and their tender pleas for her to stay. It tugged at his heart-strings, the ones he did not care to acknowledge existed, but flashes of being that ten-year-old boy who had just lost his own father came back to him. He heard sniffles from the boys and thought she was probably hugging them. He hurried back down the stairs, deep in thought. Well, he would not beg her to stay, but perhaps he might ask her nicely.

Pacing at the bottom of the stairs, he was ill-prepared for the sight, when she presently appeared, of her bathed and in an almost clean frock. She had not yet replaced the horrid poke bonnet over her shining ebony locks and her skin was of the finest porcelain colour. Miss Elliot was a ravishing beauty, and there was something disturbingly familiar about her.

He, Robert Fielding, seasoned bachelor of the *ton*, had to force his gaze away. He held out his hand to direct her to the door, where his curricle was waiting outside.

Before handing her into the vehicle, he asked, "Where would you like to go?"

She looked away shyly. "I do not know the address. I was hoping you would know."

He was suddenly attempted to place his hands around her beautiful neck and squeeze. Swallowing his bile, he looked skyward for a moment, so as to control his temper.

"Much though I am familiar with London, I do not have the entirety of Society and their addresses memorized. Whom might the lucky recipient of your person be?"

"Well, I never!" she gasped. "I believe I will make my own way, sir."

Her prim little chin jutted into the air and she turned to walk away from him. He leaned against the curricle, enjoying the outraged sway of her hips more than he should, while he pondered what he should do. She would not make it very far before turning back for help. He contemplated letting her take this course, but she was young and naïve. She could easily fall into the wrong hands, and not too far from the luxuries of Mayfair, either...especially looking as she did.

He hopped into the curricle and took the reins from his tiger. He began to follow along beside her, struggling to keep his fresh bays to a walk when they were itching to lean into their collars. She did an admirable job of ignoring him as she walked past other pedestrians and vendors. After passing two streets at the pace of a turtle, he could not help but speak.

"It is a lovely day for a walk."

His gesture was returned with what sounded like a grunt. Her face was certainly set in an uncompromising scowl. He saw her chin begin to quiver and then her shoulders slumped slightly, so he decided to try a different approach.

"Where are you going, miss? May I give you a lift?"

That seemed to snap her out of her doldrums. Her chin went straight back up in the air and she almost marched like one of his soldiers. It was all Robert could do to keep a straight face.

"I will deal quite well, I am sure."

What more could he say? He had always had a way with the ladies, but he had never had to try before. Wondering when she was going to pay attention to her surroundings and realize she was heading into the slums of St. Giles, he handed the ribbons to his tiger and jumped down to walk beside her.

"Miss Elliot, I did not mean to injure your feelings before. Please allow me to escort you to your friend's home."

She stopped and turned. "Is that supposed to be an apology?" she snapped.

"Yes, of course." Was it not—what else did she think it to be?

"It was a wretched attempt. You are not used to doing it, I can see."

"Miss Elliot, please get into the curricle. You have made your point." He held out his hand to her. "You are about to walk into the rookery and I would prefer not to defend you against thieves with no morals."

Her eyes widened in surprise. Clearly it had not occurred to her that such people existed. To make his point, he continued, "Yes, one look at you, even in your somewhat dirty clothes, and you would be forced into a brothel or worse. Conversely, you could be violated and pillaged in a dark alley and left for dead after they took anything of worth you had."

"Mr. Fielding, it is hardly necessary to be graphic," she scolded in an admirable governess' voice. However, she did take his hand and climb into the carriage.

He walked around and climbed into the other seat taking up the reins. "Now, who are these friends of yours?" he asked, noticing the sun was beginning to lower into the evening sky. There would not be too much time to go hunting for her friends.

"Penelope Foster is one of me dearest friends, and was coming to London first. She is the ward of the Duke of Blackbourne. Have you heard of him?"

Had he heard of him? Who in the kingdom had not? "Yes, I am acquainted with him. He is a naval war hero." He turned the horses around, negotiating through donkey carts, wagons, and horse traffic, then began to drive back into Mayfair, to the largest house in Town.

"Were you in the army, sir?"

He inclined his head. He did not wish to speak about those years. The only people he could talk to about it were his brothers in arms. Even then, most things were best left unsaid.

"My brother is in the army," she said quietly.

She was not alone in the world, then, Robert thought; she did have some family. Did the sibling know his sister was reduced to hiring herself out? It occurred to him that perhaps their family had fallen on hard times.

"What regiment is he with?" he asked.

"The 18th Dragoons."

Something about the way her voice cracked when she said that made him very cautious. Elliot was a common name in England, but could she be Philip Elliot's sister? The same black hair, the same blue eyes…that would change everything. It took a great deal of willpower not to curse aloud.

He slowed the horses before the gates of Blackbourne House. Unfortunately, the knocker was down. He sighed. "I am afraid the family is not yet in residence. Do you happen to know anyone else in Town?"

"I am not sure if they are here yet, either. Miss Johanna Grey and Miss Caroline Perkins are my two other friends. I do not suppose you are acquainted with either?"

"Of the Northumbria Greys?" he asked with raised brows.

"Relations, I believe," she said excitedly.

He turned and spoke quietly to his tiger, who hopped down and ran to speak to someone on the street while they waited. When he returned he gave an address in the newer part of Town. Robert told his horses to walk on, and they were off, though he was not optimistic that he would see Miss Elliot situated so easily. He began to consider the options open to him and, other than returning her to his own home, which would certainly seal their fate, there was only one person he could think of to petition for help.

As he feared, the families were not in residence at the Grey home either.

He cast a sideways glance at Miss Elliot and he saw tears pooling in her eyes, though she was struggling bravely to maintain her composure.

"Where am I to go?"

"I will not leave you on the street."

"I cannot return to a bachelor residence."

"Your virtue is safe with me, I assure you." He had not meant to be offensive, but she wrinkled her face as though he had told her she was an antidote. Why did he think taming the boys would be simple compared to her?

He therefore did the only thing he could; he drove to his aunt Phyllida's.

CHAPTER 4

*Y*ou need not be so cruel." The beastly man was obviously enjoying her discomfort, while she was facing life on the streets in cold, wretched poverty. To add to that, she knew not if her brother were alive or if he lay injured in some horrid foreign country. Therefore, she did what almost anyone with a modicum of feeling would do in her situation; she burst into tears.

"Do anything, but please do not cry." She heard him groan, and Adelaide tried to dry her tears. It was humiliation in its worst form to cry in front of this man.

"Miss Elliot!" he begged.

That only made matters worse. She inhaled painful, ragged breaths which, to her greater chagrin, became hiccups.

"For goodness' sake!"

An arm came around her and he awkwardly patted her shoulder. She was shocked into silence.

"There, there," he mumbled, "I will not leave you on the street. See, we are at my aunt's house."

He meant to leave her with a stranger? Wary, she yet took his hand and allowed him to lead her to the front door, where an old, stiff-lipped butler admitted them.

"Would you please inform my aunt that I would beg a word with her? And would you please show Miss Elliot to a parlour to wait?"

"Of course, sir." The butler spoke a few commands to one of the waiting footmen and then regally climbed the stairs.

"If you will follow me, miss," the footman said, and he showed her to a small saloon in which to sit while Mr. Fielding was saying the Lord knew what about her to his aunt.

She listened intently and heard his boots thudding as he climbed the stairs. He must be in the room above her, for she could hear someone pacing about and the deep timbre of a male voice. Resigning herself to a long wait, she looked around her.

Everything was white with gilt trim, from the carpets to the curtains, and the walls were lined with portraits of bewigged lords and ladies in court dress. Afraid to sit down for fear of soiling the upholstery, she felt very conscious of her circumstances. Never before had she been surrounded by such luxury. Aunt Hogg's country house was well-appointed, but this felt the way she imagined a palace would.

She hurried to stand behind a chair when she heard footsteps now descending the stairs. When the door opened, she looked up, feeling guilty for intruding on this unsuspecting lady.

"Miss Elliot, may I present to you my aunt, Lady Phyllida Middleton?"

"Lady Middleton." Adelaide dropped a courtesy fit for the Queen.

"Miss Elliot, I am sorry to hear of the circumstances which have brought you to London. Unfortunately, my home is being refurbished at the moment, so I cannot accommodate you here. What few rooms are available are all occupied by my staff."

Adelaide held her breath. She did not wish to be deposited with a stranger, and yet, she could not stay with him. What could she do?

The disappointment must have shown on her face. The lady's eyes were kind. "Do not fret, my dear," she said. "I will simply come to stay with you at Robert's house until your friends arrive in Town or my house is completed. It was supposed to be done a month ago," she added with a heavy sigh.

"I could not impose on you so, my lady. There must be another way."

"I do not see it this night at least. It is no trouble at all, I assure you."

"Return home, Robert, and tell your cook we will dine at eight. I will bring Miss Elliot with me when I have made ready."

"You are the best of aunts," he said, kissing her cheek. The caress brought a twinkle to her eyes and a rosy hue to her cheeks. He clearly held the lady in considerable affection. When the door closed behind him, she turned to Adelaide. "I know he is a rogue, but I do have a soft spot for him."

Adelaide was still stupefied by the last day of her life, and could not respond coherently. She was quite certain she did not like Mr. Fielding, but he had been kind enough to bring her to an appropriate chaperone—and that when he had seen the worst side of her tongue. Now she not only owed him an apology and gratitude, she would be obliged to stay in his house.

"Would you care to write notes to your friends while my maid packs my belongings? Then they will know you are here as soon as they arrive in Town." Lady Middleton walked over to a small writing desk and laid out paper and pen. "Is there anything else I may have sent to you while you wait?" Before Adelaide could answer, the lady tugged on the bell-pull and ordered tea.

"Now, my nephew mentioned you might need more clothing, seeing as you have only brought the small reticule in your hand and are wearing the gown you arrived in. It is much too delicate a thing for him to say to you, of course, but he is ever the considerate boy. Is he not?"

Adelaide nodded, feeling very self-conscious that he had noticed such a thing. Of course he would, she thought, given how immaculate his own person was. He must have been disgusted by her! Her lips cracked into a smile at the thought.

"On second thought, perhaps you should come with me and we will see what my maid can fit to you. It is too late to visit the shops today but we can attend to that on the morrow. Come along, dear."

Adelaide climbed the stairs behind Lady Middleton, thinking it was futile to resist this force of nature.

ROBERT HURRIED BACK to his town house to check *Debrett's Peerage* to see if his suspicions were correct. He dashed into the house with scarcely a greeting to his butler and into his study. Knowing its precise location, he took the book from the shelf and cracked open the rarely used tome. He flipped to the desired page as quickly as he could. Running his finger down to the name, he stopped at Elliot, Philip. His eyes moved to the right and he found Adelaide. Briefly closing them against the unwelcome truth, he slid down in his chair and rested his head on the desk with a groan.

"Why me?" he wondered aloud.

Philip had been working with him on covert operations for Wellington and had not been heard from in almost a year. Philip belonged to a group of soldiers who considered themselves brothers, and Robert had befriended most of them. The six brethren had vowed to take care of each other's families should something happen to them, yet Philip had been Robert's responsibility when he had gone missing. Allowing this to happen to Philip's sister was more a sin of omission than a deliberate error. Robert had known, in the back of his mind, that Philip had a sister at school; he had, however, failed to determine her well-being.

Closing the book slowly with a considered motion, he addressed four quick notes, before returning the book to its shelf and preparing to set forth to consult with Philip's fellow brothers. He mulled over the various options. Miss Elliot was not compromised, yet, but coming to live in his home, a renowned bachelor, even with the protection of his aunt, would still raise eyebrows.

He smiled a little at the thought. He would not lack for entertainment while she and his wards were in residence. However, he was as good as her guardian, with Philip's whereabouts unknown, and therefore under his protection. It was a pity; he would have enjoyed taming her very much, he thought with a wry twist of his lips.

Placing his beaver hat atop his head, he took his Malacca cane from Percy and began walking towards St. James' deep in thought. Anyone of his acquaintance who might have passed him would have guessed at his rudeness, so deep in concentration was he.

By the time he arrived at White's Gentlemen's Club, the major-domo held the door for him. "Good evening, sir. The other military gentlemen are here. Will you be joining them for dinner?"

"Yes, thank you," he replied, handing him his cape and hat while still pondering the best course of action.

Matthias, Colin, James and Luke—the four remaining brethren—stood cautiously when he entered the private dining room, but waited for him to speak.

"Good evening, gentlemen," he said as he joined them and sat down.

They all returned to their seats, still watching him with a certain degree of wariness. Robert had called an urgent meeting, a plea to come without delay.

"Relieve our anxieties, please, Major Fielding. Has Philip been found?" Matthias Landry, now the Earl of Thackeray, asked, staring at Robert with his piercing green eyes.

"Unfortunately, no...but his sister has."

"What do you mean?" As Colin spoke, a stray ginger curl fell onto his forehead.

"I mean, she appeared at my estate in the form of a governess for my two new wards."

"This does not look good. Not at all. Philip would never have left her in such circumstances." Luke said aloud what they were all thinking. His thick black brows were drawn together, making him look formidable.

"Precisely."

"What do you suggest we do?" Matthias asked. "He has not been declared dead."

"Not to my knowledge, no. His body has not been found, and

unless petitioned, it is several years before the courts will do so," Robert said slowly.

"Matthias, do you think you could find Philip's solicitor and see if there is any provision for Miss Elliot?" Luke asked. Matthias had studied law at Oxford despite being an heir to an earldom.

"Of course. But do you not think the solicitor would have contacted her before now if there had been any arrangement?" Mathias asked.

"I cannot presume to know. Philip was young when his commission was bought and I cannot think the man we served with would have knowingly left his sister without provision."

"Someone paid for his commission and her schooling," Colin, the quiet, observant one, pointed out. "And he did ask us to protect her."

"Indeed. Before I take it upon myself to act on her behalf, I would very much like to know what the circumstances are."

Luke whistled under his breath. "You would become her guardian? Are you certain you wish to do that? The bachelor beau?"

"Miss Elliot is not one I could leave to fend for herself, I am afraid. She has Philip's looks and his temper."

"I am having trouble picturing Philip as a lady," James quipped, and they all laughed.

"I intend to continue searching for him," Robert announced.

"My men have found nothing," Luke added.

"You still have men over there?" Robert asked with astonishment.

Luke gave a disheartened nod. "Tobin."

A waiter knocked and entered with their dinners. All picked sombrely at their steak and kidney pies with the reminder of their brother left behind, and how the war had left an indelible stamp on all their lives. They had sold out and tried to leave their demons behind them, but being fierce patriots, all were determined not to let Napoleon win in England now they were home again.

"Since none of you know any details of Philip's estate, I will continue to ensure she is taken care of," Robert remarked.

"We mean to help. We promised Philip," James explained. Luke, Mathias and Colin readily agreed.

"I must return home. With my father's recent death, the estate is in too much turmoil," Matthias answered, though Robert could see the difficulty those words cost him. "However, I can have Philip's affairs looked into."

"I am certain the four of us can manage the rest," Robert replied. "I know I am not one of your brethren, but I feel the same commitment to Philip."

The others nodded their understanding.

"Shall we meet again in two days' time? Hopefully there will be more news and together we can make a decision about what would be best for Philip's sister."

"Does she know he is missing?" James asked.

"I did not ask directly. I needed to confirm her identity, first. I think she suspects, however. I will have that difficult conversation with her when I return. She is staying at my house for the time being."

All eyes were upon him with open astonishment. "Hold hard, boys. My aunt Phyllida is there with her."

"Poor Beau Fielding," they harassed, mercilessly.

"Tease all you like, gentlemen. Aunt Phyllida intends to bring her out. You will all have your turn at escorting her about Town."

CHAPTER 5

*L*ady Middleton was like a storm that came upon you with no warning. Before Adelaide knew what was happening, she was being cosseted and fitted by a virtual army of maids. Two were draping dresses around her person and pinning them, another was attempting to style her hair, and another was laying out shifts, petticoats, silk stockings and shoes for her. The worst part was, even when Adelaide could get a word in, no one paid any attention to her objections.

She had begun to think over what had happened and let her mind wander where it would, when she suddenly realized she was being spoken to.

"I beg your pardon," she said meekly.

"Have you no family or guardian, child?" Lady Middleton repeated.

"I have a brother in the army, and an aunt, but I have not heard from her since I left for school several years past."

Lady Middleton clucked her tongue. "Who is this aunt, if I may ask?"

"Lady Hogg."

It was apparent from the scowl which appeared on Lady Middleton's face that she had no love for her aunt. Adelaide felt much the same way. It was why she had not attempted to make contact when her time at Miss Bell's was over. Aunt Hogg had made it very clear that Adelaide and Philip were burdens. By buying him a commission and sending her to school, in Aunt Hogg's estimation she had done her duty by her late brother's children.

"Well, will she not be surprised when she sees you in Society?" Lady Middleton asked with a mischievous smile.

"She is in London?"

"Every Season," the lady confirmed. "The next will begin in precisely ten days, which leaves us little time to prepare you."

"Ma'am, I am but a governess, now. I have no thoughts of the Season. I have nothing to my name. While I very much appreciate your kindness in helping me temporarily, this is too much."

"Nonsense! Your birth is excellent and you have every right to be here. Besides giving me something entertaining to do this Season, I will enjoy every moment of parading you around in front of Gertrude."

"Nevertheless, do but consider the cost, my lady! I must find a position." Adelaide shook her head.

"Do not heed the cost. It has been seen to."

"But..." Adelaide opened her mouth to protest but the lady held up a silencing hand.

"I will hear no more objections. If the Season ends and you have not made a match, perhaps then I can hire you as my companion...but I will hear no more objections for now." She gave Adelaide a stern look, and all Adelaide could do was nod in acquiescence.

She knew she would have to mention at some point that no one in their right mind would want her without a dowry, no matter how good her birth. It would fall on deaf ears at the moment.

"Now we must hurry so we are not late for dinner. I think the rose lustring will do splendidly for her tonight, Bowers," Lady Middleton said to her maid. It was one of the gowns the maids had fitted earlier, which had needed little alteration. Adelaide could not picture her ladyship in these gowns.

"These are my daughter's gowns," she said, as if reading Adelaide's mind. "She is expecting a happy event, however, and these will be out of fashion by the time she can wear them again. Fortunately, you are of a similar height and build, so we may muddle through until the modiste can finish your wardrobe for the Season." Lady Middleton hurried her from the room to dress for the evening.

Adelaide knew she should be grateful, but she felt sick. This was not to be her life, no matter how they tried to trick her out and pretend. She was still a penniless orphan who desperately needed a position. What would be expected of her for all of this? She did not want to imagine.

Soon she was dressed in a beautiful pink gown that had surely cost more then her wages for a year as a governess would have been. A matching pink ribbon was tied about her hair, which had been styled elegantly so that her curls draped about the crown of her head and also her face. Tears pooled in her eyes as she looked at herself in the looking-glass. She was deeply moved, for who could fail to be when they felt like Cinderella being tended to by a fairy godmother? However, this was no fairy tale and the clock would soon strike midnight, leaving her in rags on the cold, damp street.

Following the maid downstairs to the entrance hall, she waited to be taken back to Mr. Fielding's house, pondering what would happen next. On the short drive back, Adelaide was grateful for Lady Middleton's chatter. She did not feel up to conversation.

Adelaide did have to smile, though, at the thought of what her friends would think when they saw her. She also admitted to herself it would be wonderful to share the Season with them and be together again. When the carriage pulled up before the town house, it was the first good look at the building she'd had. Of white stone and four stories high, it spoke volumes of his position in Society. On the first occasion, she had been distracted by the boys and then, having let her temper get the better of her, had scarcely noticed. Lady Middleton's home had been lavish and opulent. Here the wealth was more subtle and understated. However, it felt more like a home then Harlton Park had, and seemed so much for one man. Should not someone with so much wealth wish to have a family and share it? Suddenly, she wondered more about who her employer was and what it said about him. She felt sorry for him.

~

ROBERT RETURNED to his house prepared to relax before the onslaught of femininity took over, for he had no delusions that any peace would remain. He had been a bachelor, living on his own, for nearly fifteen years and gave thanks daily for his solitude. Percy opened the door for him before his hand reached the knob, and the look on his butler's face told him his peace was already gone, and the ladies were not to blame.

"What have the little urchins done?"

"I think the better question would be, 'What have they not done?' sir."

Robert gave him sideways glance and waited for the news.

"First, Thomas took them to the park and Master Freddy fell into the Serpentine when chasing after the ducks."

Robert could picture the scene in his mind. It was not, after all, an unlikely event. "I trust the boy was unharmed?"

Percy nodded.

"And what was their next adventure?"

"Cook thought to let them help her bake some biscuits thinking to keep them out of mischief, but somehow they managed to break an entire shelf of crockery and spill all of the week's flour on the floor."

Robert was already envisioning the wage increases his servants would deserve for putting up with his wards. "Is there anything else?"

"Unfortunately, yes, sir. While the boys were being bathed after their kitchen mishap, Master Harry was left alone for just a moment while Master Freddy was being dried, and he decided to see if he could create waves as big as those in the sea while splashing about in the tub. I am afraid he managed enough to leak to the floor below..." The normally staid retainer averted his eyes.

Robert went at once towards the stairs on his way to the nursery, wondering why the two footmen he had assigned to the boys could not control children half their size. He paused at the next flight of stairs and went into his sitting room to fortify himself with a drink. He would not allow this temporary disturbance in his life to cause him to lose his temper. As if it was not enough that Aunt Phyllida and Miss Elliot were about to descend upon them. He made a mental note to send a large donation to Harrow in the morning. The boys had not even been in the house four-and-twenty hours. He shook his head and set down his empty glass. When he arrived at the nursery, he found his two footmen looking weary and very afraid when they spied him in the doorway. They stood to attention immediately.

"Where are they?"

The servants exchanged glances. "Asleep, sir," one whispered, his brown eyes wide with gravity.

"How was that feat managed by seven of the o'clock?" Robert asked with disbelief.

The other young footman cleared his throat. "Mrs. Simms put a little brandy in their tea, sir."

Robert almost smiled. His old nurse had used such methods at times. He would have to give his housekeeper suitable thanks, later but he would not show his admiration in front of these two young men, who should be able to handle one boy apiece.

"Is there anyone to relieve you for the night?"

"Aye, sir. Mrs. Simms has sent for some nursemaids from her sister's place, but they been asking for Miss Elliot all day."

"Then they are in luck. Miss Elliot will be here when they wake in the morning."

Robert returned to his apartments to dress for dinner. He could not remember the last time he had hosted anyone at his home for a meal. Although he rarely had dinner at home, on those occasions he took a tray in his study. Cook was delighted there would be more guests to cater to, but the other retainers showed little emotion. A collection of trunks arrived before the ladies did, so he had not imagined his folly. As far as the boys were concerned, he hoped the footmen had learned their lesson. He had sent a letter to Harrow to gain their admission and would have to keep them here and entertained at least until they were safely in residence at that hallowed institution.

Miss Elliot was another matter altogether. Philip had been directly under his command, therefore he did feel responsible for the sister's welfare. Unprepared, yet again, for the sight of her transformation when she walked through the door, at first he could only incline his head in greeting. Part of him was tempted to retreat, to walk back into Headquarters and buy his commission back. It would be simpler than the battles to be faced here at home.

Robert felt his collar tighten like a noose about his neck. He had thought her a beauty before, but now, dressed in a pale pink gown, she was a mix of the Madonna's innocence and Aphrodite's lure—a dangerous combination. He would swear she was as yet unaware of her charms. How long would it remain so?

As his eyes met hers, he felt the heat rise in the room and his pulse begin to speed. Good gracious, he could not remember that happening to him at the sight of a woman! He uttered a fervent wish that Matthias would have good news from Philip's solicitor.

Recovering his wits, he walked over to the ladies and brushed his lips lightly over his aunt's fingers. He loved making his favourite aunt blush. She pulled her hand away and wrapped his knuckles with her fan. "Behave yourself tonight, Robert."

"Forgive me, Aunt. I am unaccustomed to polite company." He turned and bowed correctly to Miss Elliot, who bobbed a reciprocal curtsy.

"Good evening, Miss Elliot. I trust you have been treated well this afternoon?"

"Indeed I have, sir. Far better than I deserve."

"I will hear none of that nonsense!" Lady Middleton chimed in.

Percy opened the door and nodded his head.

"Shall we go into dinner, ladies?" Robert offered an arm to his aunt and held the other one out for Miss Elliot. She looked at it with what might have been distaste but quickly masked her expression.

"Thank you, sir."

He seated the ladies on his right and left, a far more intimate setting then he would have liked. Thank goodness his aunt had been available to chaperone or he did not know what would have been the outcome.

"You must tell me the latest happenings, Robert," Aunt Phyllida was saying. "You have been home for two months, now, and I have only seen you once."

"Consider me duly reprimanded," he replied as he dabbed at his mouth with a napkin. There is little to tell, I am afraid. It has been the most dull time I could manage."

"That is not what I have heard," she muttered, no doubt so Miss Elliot would not hear.

He tried not to choke on his wine, and was saved when the servants placed a fricassee of veal on the table before them, along with some potatoes sprinkled with parsley, candied carrots and buttered mushrooms. "Miss Elliot, my aunt tells me you are some relation of Lady Hogg. Are you anxious to see her again?" he asked casually.

"Not particularly, sir," she answered in candid refutal. "When our parents died, she bought my brother a commission and sent me off to school, making it quite clear she had done her duty by us."

That certainly was not the response he had anticipated. "I see. Hence the reason you sought employment from me."

She inclined her head, though her eyes flashed at him.

"I realized that I am acquainted with your brother." Aunt Phyllida kicked him under the table, and in the same instant he saw Miss Elliot tense in the seat beside him. Her hand slipped to her mouth to cover a gasp.

"Do you know where Philip is?"

The look in her eyes told him everything he needed to know. He could put off speaking with her about Philip no longer.

"I am afraid not, Miss Elliot. When was the last time you heard from him?"

"I-I suppose over a year ago. He sent a letter when he was home on an errand for the Duke of Wellington."

He chanced another look at Miss Elliot and she was struggling with her emotions. Her fork was suspended over her plate as if frozen.

"I am sorry to have upset you." He uttered the platitude and was surprised to find the sentiment was genuine.

She swallowed heavily. "Do you think he is dead?" she whispered.

"I cannot say for certain. We are searching for him."

"Oh, you poor dear, this is such shocking news!" Aunt Phyllida said, eyeing Robert with disfavour, presumably for speaking of such things at the table, as she went and gathered the girl in her arms. In a peevish fit of envy, Robert wished he could be the one comforting Miss Elliot, but then chastised himself for such thoughts. Nothing could come of it, and he could hardly take advantage of a girl under his protection. He could sympathize with her fear, however, and he had known of Philip's absence for almost a year.

"I feel so helpless. There is nothing I can do but wait."

"There, my dear, there; do not take on," Phyllida comforted, as Robert silently handed the girl his handkerchief. Miss Elliot blew her nose violently, but it seemed to help her dry her tears. She dabbed at her eyes and Aunt Phyllida returned to her chair.

"Do you know anything of him? I have not had a word from anyone since." She looked at him with those enchanting blue eyes, pleading. Robert could easily become lost in those eyes, which changed colours like the warm seas of the Mediterranean...but she had asked him a question.

"Philip served under me on some special assignments, but I am afraid I have not heard or seen from him since you did."

She hung her head and covered her face with her hands. "This is what I was afraid of."

Robert boldly reached out to touch her arm. "I have not given up hope yet, Miss Elliot. There are men looking for him. Sometimes the lack of news can be good news, and it was known that he was one of Wellington's most trusted covert operators."

"Could he be in an enemy prison or lying injured somewhere?"

"I will not lie to you; it is possible. One of our fellow officers has been searching for Philip since he first went missing, and the rest of us discussed what is to be done now that Napoleon is captured."

Miss Elliot looked away.

"You do not mean to go back, do you?" his aunt asked with obvious concern.

"I do not yet know," he answered quietly.

"This is dreadful indeed! I can see by the look in your eyes that you are contemplating it." She took up her fan and waved it rapidly.

"How can I not if I am needed?" He struggled to control his temper. People who had not served in war had little idea of what it entailed—the sacrifices, the hardships, the bonds you formed with fellow men.

"I did not say I did not understand, but I hate it nonetheless."

Miss Elliot remained quiet, in all likelihood trying to absorb the shock he had given her. Perhaps she now understood why he had called his aunt to her side.

"I think I will retire, my dear. I am most disturbed and I fear will not be good company," his aunt shocked him by saying. Miss Elliot was the one he would have expected to excuse herself.

Robert rose from his chair as his aunt and Miss Elliot stood up. He escorted them to the entrance hall and wished them goodnight, feeling guilty as he watched Philip's sister climb the staircase, looking wretched with grief.

CHAPTER 6

*A*delaide barely contained her sobs long enough to make it to her bedchamber. She wanted to give in to her sorrow and throw herself across the luxurious bed, but she was too conscious of her borrowed gown. Not wishing for Lady Middleton's maid to intrude on her grief, she managed to remove the gown despite the tears streaming down her cheeks. Then she allowed herself to fall on the bed and indulge in the anguish which she had held in for so very long. There had been no privacy at school, and to have done such a thing would have been to acknowledge Philip could be gone. Perhaps too much time alone was not a good thing. Adelaide could not remember the last time she had had so much time to herself, nor allowed herself such maudlin thoughts.

Inhaling ragged breaths once her tears had slowed, she felt her grief give way to guilt. What if Philip was hurt somewhere and needed her? *'Tis a little late for that*, she thought bitterly. If only she could raise the funds to go and search for him! Then the crashing reality of it all hit her once again—she was penniless and in need of a position. Should she beg Mr. Fielding to let her remain as governess? No, he had said he would send the boys to school, and that was the best for them. She had to find a way to help Philip! Her throat began to burn with emotion again, and she blew her nose, trying to prevent another round of wailing. If only she had her friends to comfort her, not this arrogant, unfeeling oaf!

To be fair, Mr. Fielding had seemed kinder once he realized she was Philip's sister. Would he be willing to help her go to the Continent? Adelaide's mind began to race with possibilities. He had mentioned men were searching for Philip. Would he be willing to speak to her more? She would have to find out what information he and his compatriots possessed about Philip's disappearance, but she knew very little of men and how to deal with them. Miss Bell had taught them how to go on in a ballroom or grace any drawing room, but somehow Adelaide did not think Mr. Fielding would be particularly impressed by her societal manners. Her father and Philip had been gone from her for four years, and at school she had been surrounded by females.

Adelaide cried herself to sleep, but it was a restless slumber, full of nightmares where Philip lay hurt and wounded in a ditch somewhere, or was being held prisoner in a damp, cold dungeon.

"No!" she cried out. Then she sat up, soaking wet with sweat and with her sheets tangled up around her legs, breathing as though she had been running for her life. "There must be something I can do!"

"Miss Elliot, is that you?" a little voice asked sleepily.

Adelaide squinted and made out the figures of Freddy and Harry through the dim light of the dying embers in the grate. "What are you doing out of bed, boys?"

"We heard you crying and wanted to make you feel better," Freddy answered.

Adelaide was sceptical as the nursery was on the floor above, but during the night these boys looked so very young and innocent. They had been orphaned just as she had, and she felt pangs of sympathy for them. Perhaps she should do more for them before they went to school. She patted either side of her on the bed, and both boys climbed in eagerly. Putting an arm around each of them, she hugged them close.

"Were you crying because we have been bad?" little Harry asked.

Adelaide tried to think how best to answer them. "Not precisely, although you cannot continue to behave thus or Mr. Fielding will not always be so forgiving."

"But he isn't our papa!" Freddy protested.

"No," she thought carefully, "but he is who your papa chose to take care of you since he cannot."

Both boys seemed to ponder this heavily.

"So Papa will not come back if we are naughty?"

"Oh, Harry." Adelaide's throat constricted again. At least she had been old enough to understand her parents would not be not returning for her. "Your mama and papa cannot come back, though they want to very much. But they can see you from Heaven and want you to make them proud."

"I am scared," Harry said as he snuggled closer.

"Mama used to hold us like this when we were afraid," Freddy added.

"Mine did, too," Adelaide admitted, cuddling them close and thinking she would try harder to help them feel loved as she stroked their backs until all of them finally slept.

"IS THERE SOMETHING YOU NEED, Miss Elliot?" Robert watched her through hooded lids as she stood before his desk seeking an audience. She was wearing a pale blue sprigged muslin that made her eyes look like the sky and made her figure...well, he supposed it was modest, but it took very little to show her to advantage. He most definitely needed to remove himself from her vicinity for a while, especially after overhearing her conversation with the boys when he had walked past her room last night. Memories of his own struggles with his father's death at that age had flooded over him, and he had been forced to acknowledge his fault in dealing with these boys. At the very least, he should have gone to meet them and ask them their wishes.

"I know this is asking too much of you when you have already done so much." She closed her eyes and bit her lower lip for a moment, as if steeling herself to ask something awful. "If you go to look for Philip, could you please arrange for me to go with you?"

He hesitated, at first shocked by her question, then not knowing how to handle this delicate situation. He shook his head, then almost shouted, barely succeeding in controlling his temper. How could she ask such a thing of him?

"Absolutely not," he answered calmly.

She watched his face instead of responding.

"You did just ask to go with me and follow the drum to look for your brother?" he asked, as though to verify he had not misheard.

"I did. I do not know what else to do."

"No. Philip would never forgive me."

"I cannot just sit still and do nothing while my brother may need me! It was one thing not to hear from him, but to know something has happened…"

She glared at him, which he was becoming used to.

"It would quite ruin you to be under my protection." Surely she was not so naïve as not to understand what that meant?

"I am a governess, sir. There is little more can be done to ruin me now. Am I not already under your protection?"

"I must disagree. Reputation is everything to you as a governess. There is only one occupation left for you when ruined."

"You insult me, sir!"

Her cheeks took on a rosy hue when angered, and the blue of her eyes sparkled like running water. It would be so very tempting to taunt her.

"I speak the truth to you, Miss Elliot."

"If you will not help me, then I will seek the help of my friends once they arrive."

"Miss Elliot, of course you may seek the counsel of your friends," he said, his patience growing thin. "However, your brother was in a group of six men who banded together and agreed to look out for each other and their families should something happen. Philip asked them to look out for you, and he was my responsibility. I accept the blame, wholly, but I and the others intend to see you looked after as a family. Our advice comes from those who have been at war and understand the dangers that are still there."

"Is that why you took me to your aunt instead of leaving me on the street? Because of this friendship?"

"I would like to think I would have helped you regardless, but it is why I cannot allow you to chase after Philip. Luke, the Duke of Waverly, has his old batman in France, searching along with some other men. He was nearby when the ship carrying your brother went down."

"He was on a ship?" She gasped and put her hands to her cheeks. "I did not know."

"Yes," he answered solemnly. "It was not far from the coast, so we have not entirely given up hope, but many of the other passengers' bodies were found."

Tears rolled down her face and she fought hard to maintain her composure. It would have been better had she broken into loud sobs. Her valiant fight was far more disconcerting to him. She had a strength of character he was unused to in ladies of his acquaintance. Reaching forward, he put his hand on her shoulder, and was shocked when she leaned into him. Had she been alone in her fear and grief the entire time? If so, then to be cast into service and deposited in a strange home with only two wild young boys was quite an upheaval, even to his jaded sensibilities.

"Forgive me. I am still coming to terms with his disappearance," she said as she pulled back and wiped her eyes, leaving him feeling disappointed by her withdrawal. "I knew something must be wrong, but I had still hoped his letters had gone astray."

"I know how much Philip's absence has affected me; I can only imagine your feelings."

"I do not know what to feel," she admitted frankly. "He was taken from me four years ago and his letters kept us connected, but I have not had the luxury of seeing him smile in some time."

"It was as dashing as ever when last I saw it. There was not a female alive who did not swoon at the sight of it."

That drew a rich laugh from her and it was a most enchanting sound. Robert had to shake himself out of this spell she was casting over him.

"He was a rogue even as a youth," she said in wistful remembrance as she gazed off at some scene far away.

"He would want you to remember him, with us, always—not mourn and waste your own youth grieving for him. Yet we will not give up hope."

"No, you are correct. But how can I not search for him, if at all possible, when my heart tells me he is not gone?"

Robert struggled to answer her when he felt much the same. "I think your best efforts would be in sending prayers to the Almighty while we continue to do all in our power to look for him. I promise to keep you apprised if I hear anything."

"Will you take me to him if he is found?"

He gave her a long, hard look. How could he tell her the condition Philip would be in if he was found being held prisoner somewhere? "If it is possible, then yes, I will take you to him." It was the best he could offer.

She nodded, seeming satisfied. It was more than she had known or even hoped for, most likely.

"Why not try to enjoy some of the Season. Your friends will be in Town soon and hopefully that will help take your mind from worrying."

Although she gave him a quick, sceptical glance, she nodded.

"What do you intend to do with the boys?"

"I have sent a request for their admission to Harrow. I hope it will not take too long. In the meantime..." His voice trailed off.

"In the meantime, perhaps I can find diversions for them. I discovered activity first thing in the morning helps decrease their curiosity," she answered. "Along with constant supervision and locking them in their rooms with no sharp objects."

"Or pillows," he added dryly.

"Or pillows," she agreed and they shared a smile of understanding. Robert was astounded by the sensations that smile created within him. He needed to keep himself far away from Miss Elliot. The sooner she was with her friends, the better for all concerned. If they could find Philip alive… He swallowed hard. He would not give up hope, nor would he entertain false hope.

"I think I will take the boys to the Tower of London," she suggested, pulling him back from his maudlin thoughts.

"Do you think that wise?" he asked with some surprise. "It might give them ideas."

"I think it could be used to our advantage," she said, favouring him with another smile, this time full of mischief.

"Indeed?" he asked with a chuckle. She began to leave, and he was not ready for her to go. "I thought the boys might enjoy riding. Would you care to join us?"

"I have not ridden much since before I went to school, but Philip and I used to ride everywhere together."

"Then I will see you mounted for your time in London—anything to bring back good memories. I will have the carriage ready at one for the Tower…and, Miss Elliot?"

"Yes?"

"You do not need to consider yourself in my employ, but I am grateful for any help you are willing to give with the boys."

"I think they simply need reassurance and an outlet for their energies."

"That we must defeat by earning their respect," he said dryly.

A half smile curving her lips, she nodded and then left the study. Robert watched her go, and felt horrible that he had neglected Philip's sister.

CHAPTER 7

*A*delaide dressed in a plain, round gown for the outing to the Tower of London with the boys. She dearly hoped that with the aid of two footmen, she would be able to keep Freddy and Harry out of the moat or from trying out the torture devices. She had little notion of what would appeal to boys apart from the things Philip liked, which was anything to do with horses and soldiers.

After collecting the two youngsters and informing them of their outing, she could scarcely contain their exuberance and keep them from running through the house like a herd of cattle. In fact, Freddy began to slide down the banister, only to be stopped by a very stern voice.

"Master Fredrick!"

Adelaide hurried to join them and was breathing hard when she arrived at the bottom of the stairs. Mr. Fielding was leaning forward and speaking to the boys, who were standing to attention, as straight as two ramrods.

"I need your word as gentlemen that you will be on your best behaviour today. Do you understand what that means?"

"Yes, sir!"

"Please explain it to me then, Freddy, so I will feel reassured in taking you on this adventure."

"It means I will keep my word, sir."

"And you as well, Harry?"

"Yes, sir!"

"Then let us proceed. Miss Elliot?" He offered her his arm.

"Do you mean to accompany us, sir?" Adelaide watched Mr. Fielding handle the boys with ease, forcing her to acknowledge he was not perhaps the ogre she had first thought him. He had been kind this morning, and now he meant to join them for an outing to the Tower? No, it would not do. She must keep a distance and think of herself as the governess. Attaching agreeable emotions to her employer was dangerous when he was a handsome bachelor.

"Shall we go, then?" Mr. Fielding was asking as he lifted his arm towards her with a suggestion of command. In the carriage, he sat on the forward-facing bench next to her, and the boys climbed in opposite. Adelaide felt crowded and too aware of Mr. Fielding as his side touched hers in the seat. Had she ever been so self-conscious or aware of another person? When her friends touched her, it did not elicit such a response within her. As she tried to ignore these new sensations, Mr. Fielding conversed with the boys as though she were not present. Harry and Freddy were peppering him with questions about the war, which he answered with more patience than she would have believed him capable of. In his turn, he pointed out Trafalgar Square and St. Paul's Cathedral as they drove through London to the Tower.

Adelaide tried to relax and give her attention to their conversation.

"Speaking of Trafalgar, there is to be a military review in Hyde Park soon. If you have not yet left for school, we will take you to see it."

"You will?" Freddy asked with awe. "Truly?"

"If your behaviour improves, yes." He sent a knowing look at them, and the boys had the grace to flush.

"We will be the best boys ever!" Harry assured him.

"It is rumoured there will be boats in the Serpentine to recreate Trafalgar, and there will even be a fireworks display."

"Oh thank you, sir. We will be perfect!"

"No, do not promise something you cannot achieve. I do not expect you to be perfect, but I do expect you to be men of your word and behave well."

"Yes, sir!" they echoed.

When the carriage pulled up in front of the large, white stone fortress with cannons mounted along the wharf, both boys looked up with appreciation as they jumped out onto the pavement in front of the moat. A yeoman warder in a smart black and red uniform stepped forward to greet them.

"Good afternoon, I am Joseph. I will be your warder for the day."

Adelaide had not expected Mr. Fielding to come, nor had she anticipated the forethought to hire someone to show them around.

"What would you like to see first, boys? We have the menagerie, the crown jewels, the armouries or the torture devices—if your parents will allow it."

Adelaide and Mr. Fielding cast a glance at each other. She could feel her cheeks heating and Mr. Fielding did not correct the guard.

"What is a man-a-jury?" little Harry asked.

"Why it is animals. We have lions, a leopard, a bear and many other wild beasts."

"I want to see that!" Harry said excitedly.

"I wish to see the torture devices," Freddy pronounced.

"I suspected as much," Mr. Fielding retorted. "If you behave throughout the rest of the tour, we may see those at the end."

The guide took the boys in hand and Mr. Fielding offered Adelaide his arm again. She could not understand why he was treating her with such consideration. Had he and Philip been close friends and she had not known? He must have had many friends she did not know of, she thought sadly. They followed along behind the other three as they crossed the drawbridge to the Lion Tower, observing in silence. The warder would earn a handsome vail today, Adelaide suspected, for he was keeping the boys enthralled with tales of each of the animals within the menagerie. From lions, panthers, and tigers, he even spoke of an elephant that had been there in the beginning.

"What are you thinking, Miss Elliot?"

"Besides the stench? The animals are so very beautiful, but I feel sorry for them. They should be roaming the plains of Africa or stalking prey in the jungle, not confined to small cages in England."

"Then most people would never see their majesty," he argued. "King James enlarged the area for the lions so they could prowl."

"I would not think it could compare to the plains of Africa! I cannot think God would approve of this abuse." She shook her head at the occasional moans from the animals.

"Man needs to prove he is superior to other species, I am afraid."

"Climb down at once, Freddy!" Adelaide interrupted, calling sharply to the boy, who was halfway up the iron enclosure. The tiger lifted its head, but seemed largely uninterested in the boy. As Freddy promptly followed her bidding—to both her surprise and relief—she could only wonder how much taunting it would take to enrage the beast and how secure the railings actually were.

"Aye, lad. Some of the beasts will snap your hand off like you would snap a twig. We used to have monkeys running about until an unfortunate accident occurred with some boys about your age." The warder cast a knowing look at both of the boys, whose eyes had opened wide with fear.

They moved on through the dark, narrow halls and towers to the armouries, where they paused to gawk at the cache of thousands of weapons before Mr. Fielding showed the boys the uniform their father had worn when he had served under him.

Adelaide hung back, remembering her brother as last she had seen him, looking dashing in his regimentals. She stepped outside for some air, not wishing to lose her composure in front of the boys or Mr. Fielding. She had done that on enough occasions already.

They exited the building, and the boys began to run ahead to the Wakefield Tower, but a raven swooped down at Harry and frightened him. "Aaaaahhhh!" he cried. "Help!" He put his hands protectively over himself.

"You need not be afraid. The ravens are here to bring luck and protect the Crown," Joseph explained.

"This is not where people come to die, though, is it? I want to see where the executions took place!" Freddy demanded.

"You are standing in the very place. That is the scaffold," he pointed. "And it was traitors to the Crown who were executed, or thought to be." The warder murmured the last so quietly, Adelaide had to strain to catch the words.

The boys examined the scaffold in gruesome detail, and since Mr. Fielding gave it as his opinion they had earned the right they were permitted to continue and view the torture devices.

As they entered the dark, musty chamber, Adelaide had to stand back again. A gentle hand touched her back and a soft voice spoke into her ear.

"I had not considered how this might affect you. Shall I gather the boys to leave?"

"No, please do not. They would never forgive me. I am sorry if I am being silly, but it is hard not to imagine Philip…" She swallowed hard. "If I may stand back?"

"Of course. The warder seems to have them in hand."

"Yes, indeed." She smiled at him, but wished he would not stand so close. It was extremely uncomfortable to feel as though she were sharing the same space with his imposing presence. It was hard to take a breath without his scent of musk and spice invading her senses.

"It will be difficult to improve upon today's adventure," she said, averting her eyes from his person, and thus trying to encourage him to do the same. It was disconcerting, the way he always seemed to be staring at her.

"Indeed it will," he said, though his eyes were full of humour as though he had surmised her intent. "I have purchased ponies for them to ride, and I trust the grooms can keep them busy for some time."

"They have already learned to muck out the stalls, so they might even be useful," she added, forcing a slight smile.

"Every man should know how to care for his cattle," he agreed with approval. "I suppose I should hire a tutor in order for them to be ready for Harrow."

"Only if they are not accepted next term. They have a surprisingly good knowledge of reading and arithmetic. I do not think much more would be necessary at their age."

"I am impressed you were able to discover so much, given their antics in the country," he surprised her by saying.

"Harry, no!" she shouted then. While the warder was distracted by explaining the rack to Freddy, Harry was attempting to insert his legs into the manacles.

"Boys, it is past time we should return for tea," Mr. Fielding said, making it sound like a command instead of a suggestion.

The boys groaned in unison as Adelaide had expected, except they obeyed immediately by coming back to his side.

Adelaide was pleased with the success of their outing as they walked to the carriage. The boys skipped ahead, Mr. Fielding thanked and tipped the warder, and Adelaide felt the day had been worthwhile. The boys had seemed happy and appropriately curious. If only they had not tried to catch one of the ducks swimming across the moat...

"You look done for. Have a drink," Luke said, handing Robert a glass as he sat back in the Duke's study. "Having children around is exhausting, eh? Or is it Miss Elliot?"

"Both," Robert groaned. "We took the boys to visit the Tower today. Other than a swim in the moat, it went rather smoothly."

"You took the boys to the Tower?" Luke appeared stunned.

"Why? Should I not have done? I did not think it fair to send Miss Elliot alone with them, knowing their repute. Besides, they seem to respond to me." He shrugged, as if he had not done something completely out of character.

"It must be the military bearing," Luke guessed. "Then what of Miss Elliot? Is she swooning at your feet, like every other female in London?"

Robert scowled. "Not at all, in actual fact. She does not seem to be aware of me at all—at least not as a man."

Luke raised his eyebrows as though he doubted it were possible.

Robert lifted his hands. "I am completely serious. She has no feminine wiles. I can speak to her freely. It makes me want to recommend her finishing school far and wide."

Luke laughed and raised his glass in salute. "I cannot wait to meet Philip's sister. Meg suggested we invite everyone to a picnic before the Season begins. It will be more comfortable for her if she knows more people, and we can help entertain the boys for an afternoon at least."

"I am much obliged." Robert lifted his own glass in salute this time. "I think it an excellent idea. Miss Elliot does not seem too thrilled by the prospect of having a Season. She protested wildly when Aunt Phyllida whisked her away to the modiste. Perhaps she will change her mind when her friends arrive."

"I am pleased to hear she has friends, though Meg is bringing Amelia out, so she will not feel alone."

Robert whistled. "Miss Elliot and Lady Amelia in one Season. I do not know if London can handle it."

"She is as beautiful as that?" Luke questioned.

"Easily, and more besides. Imagine Philip's charm and handsomeness in a dainty little package with a fiery personality to boot."

"At least we will be able to sympathize with each other. She sounds much like Amelia with black hair. With the four of us here, hopefully we can keep the scoundrels away. With no dowry to speak of, we will need to keep a close watch."

"I know all their tricks," Robert retorted. "Speaking of dowry, I received a note from Thackeray this afternoon. It was the reason I called." He took a letter from his coat pocket and unfolded the paper.

R. Fielding Esq.,
  Sir,

THE ELLIOT SOLICITOR *has informed me that Lady Hogg was appointed temporary guardian over Philip and Adelaide Elliot until they reached the age of eighteen. Miss Elliot attained that majority in April of this year. It appears Philip has some accounts for himself and Miss Elliot, which he has been making regular contributions to, and I have applied to the bank for further knowledge of his assets. It may require going through the courts to have him pronounced dead, which I am hesitant to do at this juncture. The solicitor believes the amount set aside for Miss Elliot to be modest, but would not leave her completely destitute. I will write further when I hear from the bank.*

I REMAIN YOUR OBEDIENT SERVANT,
   Thackeray

"WELL, potentially, that is good news for Miss Elliot. Perhaps she may make a respectable match this Season and alleviate her concerns," Luke said thoughtfully.

Robert made a half-hearted noise of agreement. He was not certain he liked the sound of that, though he should be grateful to have one less obligation. Once the boys were ensconced at Harrow and she was married, he could return to his habitual way of going on.

"Do you have plans for this evening?"

Robert frowned. "I had not considered. I am rather spent." He laughed.

"Perhaps you should hire a tutor for the boys for the summer. I should be very surprised if the school will accept them before the summer holiday."

"That is what I suggested to Miss Elliot, but she seemed to think it was unnecessary."

"It sounds as though she is planning to remain their governess for the foreseeable future and not participate in the Season."

"Devil take it! I suspect you are correct." He shook his head. "Insufferable female!"

"Perhaps when she understands her circumstances are not dire, she will be more willing to take her place in Society. If necessary, we can contribute to her portion and thus ensure her dowry is adequate. She need not know it did not all come from Philip."

Robert smiled slyly. "Why did I not think of that?"

"Because you knew she would not accept it otherwise. Thankfully, Philip was trying to make provision for her. When we hear from Matthias, we can send a draft to the bank and she will never know."

"Perfect. Then I can convince her she need not be a governess."

CHAPTER 8

*A*delaide had spent the past two weeks in complete confusion. Mr. Fielding had hired not one, but two tutors for the boys, and thus she had only had peripheral involvement with them—and him. She was being treated as a guest and had even been assigned her own abigail to dress her. Lady Middleton had taken up her patronage with gusto, and now Adelaide had a wardrobe fit for a duchess, and had attended several small gatherings of the Countess's friends.

Today, they were to go to the Duke of Waverley's summer cottage in Richmond, to have a picnic and meet Philip's friends. Adelaide had not met a duke before, but he was a friend of Philip's and he might be willing to help her. It did not mean she was not terrified!

She and Lady Middleton rode in an open landau, while Mr. Fielding and the boys rode alongside. They had taken to riding and caring for the horses with creditable seriousness, and being allowed to ride beside Mr. Fielding was a reward. When Adelaide had protested at the distance, he had argued that it would be good for them and keep them occupied.

"Besides," he had added with a knowing twist of his lips, "they may always be put in the carriage should they grow tired."

When they pulled through the gates of the Duke's summer house,

Adelaide was certain this was the most beautiful place on earth. The carriageway was lined with lime trees, creating a beautiful archway, and a large fountain stood as the centrepiece of the circular drive in front of a white stone mansion. Riots of colour adorned the gardens all around the house as though an artist had taken his brush and arranged them into perfect beauty.

"Wait until you see behind the house," Mr. Fielding said in a low voice from close behind her, sending a shiver down her spine. When had he come to be there? No doubt she was gaping in a gauche manner, but beauty like this needed to be appreciated.

"I could not agree more," he said in a low, husky voice. Had she spoken out loud? She turned her head. He was looking at her, not the gardens. She could feel heat rising to her cheeks and she looked away again.

"Shall we greet our host?"

"I suppose we must. Have you met the Duchess?"

"I have, and you will adore her. Do not be afraid," he encouraged.

"Am I so obvious?"

"You are trembling," he revealed, adding in a teasing tone, "unless, of course, that is for me."

"A gentleman would not mention it." She cast him a scathing glance, and realized he was flirting with her. Why would he do such a thing? She was hardly in his style, according to his aunt. It had been very enlightening to sit through discussions about him and hear of his reputation as the bachelor beau. His aunt said he had joined the army to escape some vicious attempts to see him married, and had returned more hardened than ever against machinations to see him leg-shackled.

Society was so very different from Adelaide's imaginings. Her father had been a gentleman and the second son of an Earl, but they had not graced fashionable society. They had lived in a modest cottage in the country and had been very happy in their quiet family life.

She felt very naïve and uncertain about the upcoming Season.

What if she should be offered a good match? Would she have to accept a loveless marriage and a philandering husband?

A tall, dark-haired and handsome gentleman, with a beautiful blonde woman on his arm, stepped down out of the house to greet them. Adelaide felt intimidated and inconsequential. Only Miss Bell's training kept her from physically shrinking back.

Then the lady let go of her husband's arm and came forward, to greet Adelaide. "Welcome to Somerton! We are so pleased you could join us. I have been longing to meet Philip's sister," she said with a kind smile.

"Thank you, your Grace." Adelaide sank into a low curtsy.

"Please do not stand on formality with me. I am Meg."

"And I am Luke," a deep voice said. The Duke held out a hand to assist her to rise. "You are part of our family now and will be treated as such."

Adelaide immediately felt comfortable with these people, more so than she did with Mr. Fielding. There was something about him, about his manner, which confused her.

"Please call me Adelaide or Addy as my friends do."

"Come and meet everyone. They have been anxious to greet you as well." The Duchess put her arm through Adelaide's and walked her through the house to a terrace which held a glorious view of the River Thames. A pavilion had been placed on the grass to cover tables holding food, and nearby there was a life-sized chess set which was already occupying the boys and their tutors. At a safe distance, a cricket pitch had also been marked out on the enormous lawn.

Three gentlemen and a young red headed lady of quite celestial beauty came forward to be introduced.

"Lord Thackeray, may I introduce Miss Adelaide Elliot. Adelaide, this is Matthias." Meg made the first introduction.

Another tall, broad shouldered gentleman bowed deeply to her with a twinkle in his bright green eyes. "The pleasure is mine, Miss Elliot. I cannot believe that Philip looks so good as a lady. It was worth the trip."

Everyone laughed heartily, even Adelaide.

"This is Colin Stewart, our token Scot. He only pretends to be quiet." That large, ginger-haired gentleman looked daggers at his friends but he made her a deep bow before taking her hand and kissing it.

"At your service, my lady," he said with a deep Scottish brogue.

"And this, is my sister, Lady Amelia Blake. She will also be coming out this Season."

"I am delighted, Miss Elliot." They both curtsied.

Lady Amelia then slipped her arm through Adelaide's and stole her away from the rest of the group. "I am so grateful to have another female to speak to! I mean, Meg is my sister, but she is breeding," she whispered confidentially.

"Oh! I did not know."

"No one does yet...and then there are all these men." She cast an exasperated glance over her shoulder.

"Yes, I see. They were all fellow soldiers with my brother, I understand."

"They take their brotherhood very seriously, you know."

Adelaide shook her head.

"You do look very like him," Lady Amelia said, taking Adelaide's measure with her perspicuous gaze.

"You know Philip?"

Lady Amelia smiled wistfully. "Very briefly, but he made quite an impression."

Adelaide grinned. "It would seem so."

"I do hope they find him soon. Luke has men searching for him."

"Yes, and I am grateful. If only we had received some sign of his being alive. I feel it in here, but is it enough?" She made a fist over her heart. "I feel sure I would know if he were truly gone. I wish I could go and search for him. It is so hard to try to enjoy myself whilst knowing he could be hurt or being tortured in a prison somewhere."

"Luke does not think he is being imprisoned. He said they released all the prisoners some time ago and that Tobin has searched every stronghold."

"Tobin is his man?"

"Oh, yes. He is very capable. He rescued me, you know."

"I did not," Adelaide replied with wonder.

"I am not supposed to speak of it, but you are one of us now," she whispered confidentially. "It is a very long story, but my uncle plotted to marry Meg off to a very bad man and steal her away to America. When he could not have her, he kidnapped me. It was Tobin who rescued me before we could set sail."

"How horrible!"

She nodded. "It was straight after that when your brother went missing. He was escorting my uncle to prison when a storm wrecked the ship."

Adelaide bit her lower lip to fight her emotions, but her chin still quivered.

"I am sorry, I did not mean to upset you." Lady Amelia placed a comforting hand on Adelaide's arm.

"Do not be sorry. I needed to know. I knew some of what you told me. Yet how can not I do anything to help him?"

"I have asked myself the same question. Luke and Tobin are very capable, as is Major Fielding. He worked covertly with your brother, not that I really comprehend what that signifies. Even though he is not one of the official brothers, it is evident he cares very much."

"It would seem so. As soon as he discovered who I was, he has taken great care over my reputation." If only he had cared thus for his wards, she thought sourly. Although, truth be told, that was unfair. He was caring for them now that he understood the need.

"Yes, you will have more family than you care to own by the time the Season is over, I am sure." She laughed, and Adelaide was not certain if she was comforted or frightened.

"They intend to introduce both of us together, at our ball next week. Will your friends be in Town by then?"

"I do not know. I have only heard from one of them."

"Meg sent them invitations. I would expect them to attend."

Adelaide could not believe what she was hearing. A duchess intended to introduce her at a ball and her friends would be there?

~

"It appears Adelaide and Amelia have become fast friends," Robert remarked, taking a polite sip of lemonade although he abhorred the stuff as they sat in chairs enjoying the lazy afternoon.

"I knew they would." Meg smiled and glanced across the terrace to the two girls, who were standing with their heads close together.

"It looks as though your wards are doing well, Fielding," Waverley observed.

"Indeed. The only time they seemed out of sorts was when they thought Miss Elliot was leaving."

"Perhaps that is a sign, Robert."

"Do not be ridiculous," he retorted. "I cannot credit that my best friends are scheming to see me wed. Do not make me avoid you, too."

"Nonsense. You have not taken your eyes from her all afternoon."

"I did not say she was not beautiful. I have always had an eye for beauty."

Luke snorted.

"I shall say no more," Meg agreed. "Shall we play cricket? Ladies against gentlemen?"

"I do not think that is a good idea in your condition, my love," Luke said with a disgustingly tender look at his wife.

"I am not so delicate," she scolded. "Very well, then, one of the boys may run for me if necessary."

Robert restrained himself from making a remark.

"You need not gape in such a fashion, Fielding. Their father was the top bowler four years running at Cambridge. He had no sons, so he passed his skill onto his daughters."

"Very well." Robert stood and removed his coat.

The others soon followed suit and Lady Amelia and Miss Elliot returned from their stroll to see what was happening.

"A cricket match? How delightful!" Lady Amelia clapped her hands and began to tie up her skirts as all of the men stole glances.

"Do you play cricket, Miss Elliot?" Waverley asked.

"Why, yes, sir. Miss Bell was a proponent of all forms of exercise and activity. When he was home from school, Philip used to drag me out to play."

"Excellent! Each team can take one of the boys, and the ladies may bat first."

"I am not certain that is a good idea," Luke warned.

"Nonsense. This is just for fun," Robert said, wondering why his friend was not being chivalrous.

Robert saw Meg and Amelia exchange knowing smiles. Then he saw Miss Elliot covertly trying to pin up her skirts with a hat pin. She possessed a pair of very shapely calves and he was extremely intrigued as they walked out to the field. It was a shame, he mused, that ladies had to hide their charms beneath their skirts.

Harry joined the ladies, and Meg stepped up to bat first.

"Perhaps you would care to have one of the gentlemen on your team?" Robert asked in a deliberately derogatory manner. They surely did not believe they had a chance of winning? His question was met with unladylike scowls from the Duchess' team.

"Why do you not bowl me a really gentle ball?" Meg taunted.

"Not a hope," Robert said as he released the ball.

It did not matter. Meg took a swing and cracked the ball so hard it went beyond the boundary they had set.

Robert looked at her in astonishment. She smiled sweetly and then glanced at Luke. "See, my dear, I do not need a runner."

"No, my love, as usual. Your turn again."

Meg hit the ball again and it was fielded by Captain Frome and she changed ends with Amelia.

Amelia batted next and she made a deliberate show of flaunting her well-turned ankles.

"For that, I will pitch a soft one," Robert said, flirting wickedly. This was more familiar territory and he sympathized with Luke. He did not envy him having to bear-lead Amelia through the Marriage Mart.

Amelia made contact and lobbed the ball up into the air, but Robert caught it before it landed on the ground.

"Out!"

Amelia scowled at Robert. "That was ungentlemanly!"

"Sorry, dear lady," Robert teased.

She untied her skirts and turned away with a dramatic huff of disgust.

Next to play was Miss Elliot and looking fierce, she stepped up to the wicket. Robert did not know if she was intimidated or about to take his head off. He rather enjoyed her when she was cross—perhaps too much, he thought, suppressing the smirk which sprang to his lips.

She lifted a mocking brow at him. Had he been gawking or had she caught his smile? He prepared to bowl and threw the ball hard and flat. She would not thank him for treating her as less than an equal. However, he was not prepared for the ball to come back equally hard and flat—straight into his face—knocking him to the ground.

The next thing he knew, he was blinking up into the worried blue eyes of Miss Elliot. She was holding something cold to his face. It was then he remembered what had happened.

"You hit me," he slurred drowsily. He must have passed out. How mortifying!

"I did not mean to, you wretch!" she protested. "And here I have been worried sick about you!"

"You are beautiful when you are angry."

"Wonderful! I have also damaged your brain!" She made a noise of disgust and tossed the ice down. Robert groaned in pain.

She turned and exclaimed. "Oh! Did I hurt you again? I am sorry but you should not vex me so! Do you need more spirits?" She took a glass and held it to his lips.

"No, I think someone has given me quite enough." He moved to brush it away, but somehow managed to grab her hand instead splashing some of the spirits on his shirt. Their eyes met and held, and Robert began to think she must have hit him very hard indeed. He stared at her lips with the one eye he could see from, and she seemed not only to be breathing heavily but also unable to move.

A throat cleared. "I beg your pardon, but do you think he is recovered enough to return to the house? Lady Middleton is growing concerned," Luke said. The scoundrel was clearly trying not to laugh.

"I will recover; only my pride is bruised." He blinked several times, trying to clear away the fog caused by the spirits.

"I would say more than that," Miss Elliot murmured.

Luke held out a hand and assisted him up, and he found his head was spinning.

"Steady, boy," Luke said, holding Robert still while he regained his bearings. Then they walked slowly back up the hill to the terrace, where the fielding team had already gone to take refreshment. "We were just about to carry you to the house."

"That is quite some black eye!" Harry exclaimed.

"It is no more than he deserves for taunting the ladies," Amelia jested.

Robert grunted and hoisted the ice back up to his throbbing face.

"You need a raw beefsteak on it! Oh dear, it will not be gone in time for the opening ball," Lady Middleton fretted.

"Perhaps it will keep the vermin away," he snapped.

"I doubt that. You look as dashing as ever," James said in his best débutante voice while fluttering his eyelashes.

"I suppose you would like one to match?" Robert attempted to glare at James, who only laughed.

"Maybe later, Fielding. It would be unsporting to fight someone already injured." This drew chuckles from everyone except Miss Elliot. She was sitting quietly, staring out at the river. Why would she miss her chance to poke fun at him? Dratted females. He would never understand them.

"I want to know if her aim was true," Colin drawled, causing Miss Elliot to look up. "If so, I want to know what Fielding did to set her back up."

This drew a naughty smile from Miss Elliot. She cast a glance at him before turning to Colin. "That, sir, I shall never tell."

CHAPTER 9

*S*omething had changed inside Adelaide when Mr. Fielding had looked up at her and called her beautiful—except she knew he did not really mean it. He had been inebriated from the spirits his friends had given him...and yet, she still felt differently, despite not wanting to. Since that moment, she had reminded herself frequently of his insufferable behaviour when she first met him—no, she corrected her teeming thoughts, before she had even met him. When they had returned from the picnic, she had done her best to avoid him, and he also seemed to be avoiding her. They had not seen one another since—except in her cursed mind. She could not stop thinking about him. Was his face healing? Was he angry with her? Did he think of her at all?

It was time to dress for the ball, and she was loath to go where she did not belong. Maybe she would wear a fine dress, and maybe she had pretty manners, but it did not mean she should be there. Everyone would know soon enough that she was an orphan without funds or consequence, and Society marriages were all about connections and wealth. Adelaide also did not like being used as a pawn in a game to bait her aunt. Her aunt may be a nasty, self-righteous, selfish prude, but it was not Adelaide's nature to be spiteful just to be spiteful. There had to be a good cause.

She sat heavily on the stool before the dressing table, waiting her turn for the maids to descend upon her and make her look like a princess, if nothing like the poor governess she was in truth.

The bright side of the day was the news her friends were to be there. She had received notes from Penelope, Caroline and Johanna, and felt comfort in knowing she would have more than one friend present. Lady Amelia was delightful, but where she relished male attention, Adelaide shied away from it.

When she was at last deemed suitable to attend a Society ball, she met Lady Middleton in the entrance hall to drive the short distance to the Duke of Waverley's London home for the dinner which was being held before the ball.

"You look perfect, my dear," Lady Middleton said as she surveyed the pale blue jaconet muslin gown with a silver over-dress of Honiton lace, with long gloves to match and an appropriately demure string of pearls.

"Thank you, you have outdone yourself. I am certain I have never owned, nor will own, anything so fine again."

"Nonsense. Robert will have to fend off unwanted suitors, and I shall quite enjoy watching the spectacle. Let us go now," she said, accepting her wrap from Percy and Adelaide did the same.

"Is Mr. Fielding not joining us?" Adelaide asked, as he was nowhere to be seen.

"He will meet us there. He had some unexpected business to attend to." She clicked her tongue in disapproval as they made their way into the carriage.

Adelaide admitted disappointment to herself. She had hoped to gauge her appearance by his approval when she walked down the stairs. Chastising herself for allowing her imagination to run wild and into hurtful territory, she determined to think no more of him in such a manner. Was he not the self-proclaimed bachelor beau? Had he not gone to war instead of marrying? Why would he single her out over the eligible and wealthy young ladies he could choose?

"I do not expect too many of the unsavoury sort of person to be in attendance at a ball as select as Waverley's. He must also have a care for Lady Amelia's prospects, you know, as well as yours," Lady Middleton said once she was settled in the carriage.

"It is still difficult for me to comprehend why everyone believes themselves obligated to me," Adelaide said with dismay. No matter how often she had tried to discover the reason, she had always left the question unanswered.

"Besides being gentlemen, my dear, they formed a bond of brotherhood on the battlefield. It is best not to try to understand, but if Philip asked them to look after you, then they would do anything, including give their lives, for you."

"But they do not know me," she protested.

"They do now." She waved her hand dismissively. "But that is neither here nor there. Ah, we have arrived. No matter what, always maintain a smile, my dear."

The door to the carriage opened and Mr. Fielding stood ready to hand them down.

Adelaide's wretched heart betrayed her as its beat increased to a wild staccato and her corset began to squeeze the breath from her lungs. Cursed, cursed heart! Why could it not be in harmony with her mind? Such misguided feelings could only lead to a brutal flaying later. Having handed Lady Middleton from the carriage, he poked his handsome head through the doorway to smile at her. She sat completely still on the luxurious velvet squabs, thinking it would be much more comfortable to stay where she was for the evening. There was little likelihood of her not making a fool of herself if she left the carriage.

"Come, Miss Elliot. There are several young ladies most anxious to greet you." He held out his gloved hand and she reluctantly put hers in his, knowing what would happen. The flood of tingles would rush through her body and cause all prudent thought to be drowned.

"Miss Elliot?" he asked gently, his voice full of concern. "Are you feeling well? Are you beset by nerves?"

How could she admit she was afraid of being near him? She could not. Instead, she nodded her head and swallowed. "Yes, I am feeling a little nervous."

"I will be here to guide you, as well your friends. Only a select few guests have been invited for dinner."

That was what she was afraid of. Nonetheless, she took his hand and managed to survive the feeling of turning into marmalade during the descent from the luxurious town chariot.

"You look beautiful," he said, studying her from head to toe.

"You said that once before, but you had a head full of spirits."

"And of swollen nose and eye," he agreed dryly. "It did not mean I was untruthful."

"You are healing well," she said as she looked up into his face, which was a mistake. Her mouth went dry and her knees wobbled. "We should go in," she said hurriedly, turning away from him as they made their way up the white stone steps into the mansion. She tried not to notice his scent, which was already becoming familiar, or the sense of his overwhelming masculinity. With her hand on his arm, and when her skirts brushed his leg, his latent power and manliness were impossible to avoid.

"Before I miss my chance, may I request your hand for the opening dance? I am afraid Waverley will open the ball with Lady Amelia."

"I would be delighted, sir. Thank you." *I will also be scared out of my wits,* she said silently to herself. Of course, he had to dance with her. It would look poor if he did not. He was doing his duty, she reminded herself, as he led her into the drawing room where the other guests awaited.

"Adelaide!" She heard Penelope, then Johanna and then Caroline exclaim before they rushed towards her. Temporarily, she forgot Mr. Fielding and hastened to greet her especial friends. Each of them embraced, and then they began to pepper her with questions about her presence in London.

"Lady Amelia has been telling us your story," Johanna said quietly. "Is Lady Middleton to bring you out?"

"I cannot believe you did not mention how handsome your employer is!" Penelope chided.

"Is your brother really missing?" Caroline asked.

"It is such a romantic story, that all these gentlemen are taking care of you," Johanna added.

Adelaide did not know how to answer any of it. She would doubtless feel the same way, were one of them in the same situation, but she felt overwhelmed.

"Yes, it is all true. I cannot wait to hear how all of you have been." Adelaide smiled and accepted Mr. Fielding's arm when, moments later, he came over to escort her into dinner. She did not miss the curious glances her friends exchanged as she walked away.

ROBERT COULD NOT WAIT for this torture to end. During dinner, he had watched Miss Elliot from the other end of the table, taunting him with her unassuming smiles and laughter, and now he had to do the pretty with her on the dance floor. If she was not gone from his house soon, he would lose his wits.

She had avoided him since the picnic, which intrigued him. Did not all women like to be told they were beautiful? He was not used to being ignored by the female sex. That must be what had caused this fascination with her. It was a lowering thought, that he would only be interested because she had piqued his pride.

He had not missed the interested glances which the men were casting in her direction, though to be fair, her friends and Lady Amelia were also garnering attention. Robert hated being a part of the game where females threw out lures—more oft than not falsehoods—to men and then, once the poor fools were chained for life, allowed their true characters to show.

"You should not stare at her as though she were a savoury piece of beefsteak," his aunt Phyllida chastised as she glided up beside him.

"I was just thinking about the great spectacle people will make of themselves on the Marriage Mart, only to reveal a deceitful nature after the vows are said."

"Indeed, I would agree that is often the case, but I am of the opinion Adelaide is genuine in her character. We have had the good fortune to know her in a much more personal way, living in the same house for some weeks."

He scoffed. "I suppose that is true, but what has it to say to anything?" He looked down at her with a lifted brow and mock haughtiness.

"Do you deny you are tempted?" She ignored his look. "You should stop staring at her as though you wish to kill anyone else who so much as looks at her."

"Tempted yes, but not in the way you hope."

She let out a noise of disgust as she watched the influx of guests. "Oh, dear. I see Lady Hogg. I had not thought to see her here tonight. Let us hope she does not embarrass Adelaide. I am glad to see she is surrounded by her friends from school."

"I thought you were anticipating a great row with the old harridan?"

"Matrons of the *ton* do not row, Robert. We thrust and parry with careful words and skilful manoeuvres. It is more akin to a thrilling game of chess." She jabbed him with her fan.

"This is why I avoid all of it."

"Come, let us draw closer in case Adelaide has need of us."

"As you wish."

While they made their way through the crowd of the *ton's* elite, Robert doubted Lady Hogg would be so vulgar as to confront her niece in any way other than a coldly civil greeting. What reason would she have for doing otherwise? Should she not be glad to be relieved of responsibility for her? And what, precisely, did Lady Hogg think would become of her niece after she had completed her schooling?

Robert saw the exact moment Lady Hogg noticed Miss Elliot, and he turned in time to catch sight of his aunt Phyllida gleaming with satisfaction. "The dancing should begin soon," she remarked.

Robert heard the faint sounds of the orchestra tuning their instruments as if they had heard his aunt's declaration.

They were within hearing distance when Lady Hogg stepped forward and approached the group comprising Miss Elliot and her friends. Miss Elliot had not yet noticed her aunt and looked faintly surprised when she recognized her, although she maintained her composure. Robert could only wonder what it must be like to be orphaned and have your last relative want naught to do with you. He, at least, was very fortunate in his family. His aunt and uncle had taken him in when his father had died, and even now he knew he could call upon them for anything at all, as he had when Miss Elliot had arrived on his doorstep.

"Lady Hogg." Miss Elliot curtsied. "May I introduce you to my friends from school? This is Miss Penelope Foster, Miss Johanna Grey, and Miss Caroline Perkins."

The lady inclined her head but looked vexed.

"May I have a word with you in private, Miss Elliot?"

"The dancing is about to begin, my lady," Miss Elliot said as her friends withdrew, their reluctance evident, leaving her with Lady Hogg. The three young ladies must be aware of the connection and be protective of their friend, he mused—an emotion foreign to him, yet which he was suddenly feeling.

"What are you doing here, niece?" The lady sneered in a deprecating manner.

"It is lovely to see you as well, Aunt. I was not certain we were admitting any connection," she replied, with a pleasant smile in stark contrast to her aunt's scowl.

"How did you come to be here? I made it clear I would bear no further responsibility once you had finished your schooling."

"Did you think I had arrived at a ball expecting you to bring me out?" Miss Elliot laughed. "I did not understand you to mean I was not allowed in London."

Lady Hogg's face turned red and she seemed to take a moment to survey the beautiful gown her niece was wearing—and perhaps to register the fact she was an invited guest of the Duke of Waverley.

"Did you think the name on the invitation was another Miss Elliot?"

"I did not notice. The Duchess of Waverley is introducing you?"

"They are friends of Philip's, as are Mr. Fielding and Lady Middleton. They have been most kind and gracious, so much so as to give me a Season."

"You mean to publicly shame me, then?"

"If you had behaved honourably, there would be no shame," Robert remarked, stepping forward and taking Miss Elliot's arm. "Shall we dance?"

"I would be delighted, sir." The relief she felt was palpable as they moved away, but he still felt her trembling.

As Robert led Miss Elliot to the dance floor, it was clear she had not relished the confrontation with her aunt.

"Thank you," she said. "I am sorry you had to witness that, but I thank you, nonetheless."

"There is no need to apologize. She is a spiteful woman and I have no notion how she came to be invited. We will need to be more select in the invitations we choose to accept."

"We?" Miss Elliot shook her head. "She was correct. I do not belong here."

"She has not the authority to make that determination. The *ton* will know of your relations soon enough and know she abandoned you. I care not for Society's rules and live by my own. I find I am quite content. You will be much happier when you learn to ignore them also."

"It is easy for a wealthy bachelor of good family to say such things, sir. As you have pointed out before, my reputation is all I have."

He inclined his head. "Very well. If you do not think a Duke, an Earl, my aunt, myself and all your friends have the power to preserve your reputation over one bitter old lady's, then perhaps you are right."

"That is hardly fair. I was only trying to prove a point," she countered.

"You were feeling sorry for yourself. Now, smile and show her she will not ruin your night or your Season."

"You arrogant oaf," she said with a caustic smile, bringing the fire to her eyes and the flash to her cheeks that he knew it would.

Instead of sulking, Miss Elliot showed her pluck. She held her chin up and smiled as though she had not a care in the world. Robert knew better, and he wanted to take those cares away.

When the dance was over and the Duke came to claim her for the next set, Robert knew her success was assured. Along with her new dowry, her connections and beauty would ensure a successful match.

CHAPTER 10

*Y*ou must not allow him to affect you so. Simply ignore him. Trust me, my dear," Lady Middleton said when the Duke of Waverley led Adelaide back to her chaperone before the next set.

Adelaide was too shocked to speak. Had her ladyship overheard her conversation with Mr. Fielding?

"I am sure I do not know what you mean," Adelaide replied, trying not to blush.

Lady Middleton's gaze was too knowing and she merely smiled. "Robert has that effect on most ladies. If you are immune, you are unique. Here come your friends. Are you engaged to dance the set? Not yet... Very well, then perhaps you should sit it out and speak with them."

"Yes, we have much to discuss."

"So long as it is only one set," Lady Middleton said as she drifted away to greet an acquaintance.

"Come, Adelaide," Penelope said. "We are kidnapping you for the duration of this dance. We must know everything. I cannot bear to continue guessing."

Johanna and Caroline followed them to a small alcove fitted with a bench seat and chairs, and they gathered into it for a cose.

"There is really very little more to tell," she began as they settled their skirts and huddled together for the story. "Mr. Fielding was—is —my employer and he is a bachelor. He inherited two wards, who are rather wild, and when they accidentally set Harlton Park on fire, I brought them to London. It so happens that Mr. Fielding was Philip's commanding officer, and when he discovered who I was, he insisted on treating me as a lady, providing me with not only a chaperone, but a Season as well."

"How incredible!" Caroline exclaimed. "It sounds like a fairy tale."

Adelaide shook her head. "No, there is no happily ever after here, but they hope I might make a respectable match."

"What of Mr. Fielding? He is remarkably handsome and well situated, I hear," Jo asked, ever pragmatic.

Adelaide laughed derisively. "He is that, but he is insufferable, besides having the self-proclaimed intention of remaining a bachelor for life."

"He looks at you as though he is reconsidering," Jo said.

"We do not rub along well together. Please do not look for anything in that quarter."

"If you say so," Caroline said with a shrewd smile. Adelaide cast her gaze heavenward and would have been annoyed, but she had missed her friends too much.

"We must meet again soon. There is too much to say for just one dance. Have any of you secured any prospects yet?" Adelaide asked to divert the subject from herself.

"We have just arrived. There has been no time for matchmaking."

"Then who is that handsome gentleman you were dancing with, Penelope?" Adelaide asked.

"My guardian, the Duke of Blackbourne."

"He is your guardian?" All three twisted their heads about and looked at her with disbelief.

"That is a very long story. Do not set your sights in that direction for me, either," Penelope warned. We must plan a tête-à-tête. Will you be staying with Lady Middleton?" Jo asked.

Adelaide could feel her cheeks heat. "Actually, we are staying at Mr. Fielding's house. Lady Middleton is having work done."

"You are still his governess?" Caroline asked.

"No. Perhaps I should look for somewhere else to stay. It does look rather particular for me to remain at Mr. Fielding's home, even if his aunt is there."

"I would not be concerned, if I were you. From the looks of things, you may be offered a permanent residence there very soon," Caroline predicted.

"Caroline," Adelaide said in a warning voice and her friend only smiled mischievously at her.

"Of course, you are welcome to stay with me," Penelope offered. "Blackbourne House certainly has enough rooms!"

"Is Lady Ashby treating you well, Caroline?" Adelaide asked. Caroline had agreed to be Lady Ashby's companion in exchange for her chaperonage.

"Well enough," she replied vaguely.

"As long as you are able to enjoy the Season and not be her drudge the whole time."

"What of your prospects, Jo? Are you still determined to remain a spinster?" Caroline asked, also deflecting the questions on to one of the others.

"There is nothing wrong with being a spinster," Jo replied, defending her inclinations. She nodded her head subtly towards Adelaide, but the latter still noticed.

"You do not need to watch your tongues in my presence. However, I am not sure what is best to do." Without thinking, she worried her bottom lip.

"You know you always have our support if you need us, Addy." Penelope reached over and placed a comforting hand on her arm.

Captain Frome was walking towards her. She had promised a dance to each of those brethren present. The Captain had a dry wit and she had enjoyed her brief acquaintance with him, so she did not mind that Philip's friends were being overly protective.

He walked up to the four of them and bowed. "I am not sure my heart can take so much beauty in one picture."

Adelaide laughed. "Friends, behold Captain James Frome."

"Captain Frome, these are my dear friends, Johanna Grey, Carolyn Perkins, and Penelope Foster."

"Half-pay officer, rogue and flirt at your service," he said with a delicious smile and a wink. "I have come to claim my dance." He held out his arm to Adelaide and practically swept her off her feet into the waltz that was starting.

"Are you going to behave, Captain?"

"As much as I ever do." He pulled her into a turn, and surprised her with his adroitness. He was also holding her closer than the dancing master had said was proper, and she looked up at him with a questioning gaze.

"What are you about, sir? This is my first dance and you are holding me far too close for propriety," she scolded.

He laughed.

"Would you have me labelled as fast at my first ball?"

"You are adorable when you are in spirits," he said simply. "Smile and pretend you are enjoying yourself."

"I am enjoying myself, but I should still like to know if you are up to some mischief or other. Philip used to get the same naughty look in his eyes."

Captain Frome looked away for a moment, as if he were in another place entirely, before smiling and returning his attention to her. "Philip and I used to get into some exceptional fixes with the ladies."

"I can certainly believe it," Adelaide quipped.

"Very well, then. I have decided to court you," he pronounced.

"Do not be ridiculous." She instantly dismissed his words as tomfoolery.

"I should be deeply wounded by your response, but instead I have a plan." He gave her a wink full of roguish promise.

"Oh, no," she groaned.

"Oh, yes, Miss Elliot. Since you do not know Major Fielding as I do, you may not realize how his behaviour gives him away. He thinks to be a martyr on the battlefield of bachelorhood, and his friends have decided to open his eyes to the futility of it. Much like the battle with the Americas, it is pointless; nevertheless, he is intent on resisting your charms."

"Are you expecting me to thank you?" she asked with heavy sarcasm. "What if this battlefield does not wish to be conquered?"

"Also futile," he replied amiably. "You are as obvious as he is, my dear. Even now his gaze follows you as he glowers. It is a delightful thing to witness. However, he must realize he needs you."

"I am a governess with no prospects. Even were he to be attracted to me, his good sense would prevail in the matter."

"Nonsense! Fielding has no need for your prospects, as you term them, and you do have a dowry. Have you not been told?"

Adelaide almost tripped as her confusion clouded her awareness. His hand tightened on her waist while the bulk of his muscled frame guided her through the next few steps until she recovered. She must have shaken her head.

"I was told you have five thousand pounds. Certainly not enough to brand you an heiress, but sufficient to be respectable."

"How did you come to hear such a thing?" she asked in complete disbelief.

"One of the brethren contacted your brother's solicitor. I presumed you knew he had been putting something aside for you." The dance ended and he led her back to Lady Middleton. Adelaide's mind was whirling. If this was true, then she could travel to the Continent to look for Philip.

"I will call on you tomorrow," he said with a grin and another unsubtle wink as he bowed.

～

ROBERT WATCHED James flirt with Miss Elliot and his blood began to boil. James was as big a rogue as he was himself! Then Robert laughed. "By Jove! I do believe I am jealous!"

"What is so amusing?" Luke asked, walking towards Robert with a glass of wine in his hand.

"I was just observing how absurdly James is making a cake of himself."

Luke eyed him keenly and thankfully changed the subject. "Miss Elliot has that effect on most men, it seems," he said. His gaze followed her as a court of men surrounded her and her friends the moment the dance ended.

Robert had noticed, but he only inclined his head. He was still trying to assimilate the fact that he cared.

"Miss Elliot was asking a lot of questions when I danced with her."

Robert's brows lifted. "I assume this is relevant to me?"

"She was asking about Philip. It is natural for her to be interested, but her questions seemed to be more specific, as if she were formulating a plan to try to find him herself."

"Silly chit! What does she think she can accomplish on her own? I told her people were looking for him."

"Yes, I am, as you well know, and she therefore asked me. I told her everything I could—that Tobin had searched all of the known prisons and every house within fifty miles of the coast where the ship wrecked."

"Where can he be, dash it?" Robert might have punched something if he were not in polite company.

"I wish I knew. I do not know how much longer to keep searching for him. Mayhap my instincts are wrong." Waverley shook his head.

"Then our instincts are all at fault. We all have the feeling he is still alive."

"As does Miss Elliot, it seems. When I left her with Lady Middleton, she was contemplating going to Vienna to speak with Wellington."

Robert groaned. "Why must I acquire not two, but three wards? If only I had dealt satisfactorily with the boys before she arrived."

"Were it not for the boys, we might not have found her. Meg and I would be happy for her to stay with us if it would ease your mind. I think it would ease Meg's burden with Amelia if she had a companion her own age."

"My aunt would object to that, I suspect," Robert said carefully, contemplating how he felt about it as well.

"Then I hope, for your sake, that she is married quickly and becomes someone else's problem. However, we will still help whenever she needs us."

Robert was watching a group of men, including James, make fools of themselves over Miss Elliot, and he caught Luke considering him with an amused smirk.

"I have a feeling you did not hear much of what I just said. It looks as though James will be happy to take up her cause—if you do not call him out first." Luke slapped him on the back and walked away, laughing.

Robert knew he was brooding, but he did so anyway. He had a feeling Miss Elliot meant to do something rash, and he wished he knew enough of how her mind worked to anticipate it. There was little she could do without money, and he had not told her of the dowry set aside for her yet. Thankfully, he, Waverley and Thackeray had been named as trustees and she could not access it without their permission. He had done this so no scoundrels could take advantage of her, but perhaps it would turn out to be for her protection from doing something foolish. Could she not see how dangerous it would be to go to the Continent alone? Tobin had been searching for almost a year with the backing of the army and the funds of a duke. In no time at all, she would go through the money she had and be left with nothing to live on.

"Robert, my dear, you really must dance with some other ladies, unless you wish to cause talk. Miss Elliot's three friends are newly arrived in Town and quite eligible," Aunt Phyllida suggested.

Robert was a gentleman. Even though he hated the Marriage Mart, he knew he should dance with Miss Elliot's friends. Perhaps he could even draw some information from them. He pushed away from the marble column against which he had been leaning. "Very well. Who do you suggest first?"

Following the opening dance with Miss Elliot, he had danced with Lady Amelia and her vivacity was enough to make his head explode. He hoped the other three young ladies were a little more subtle. This Season could not be over fast enough for his liking.

CHAPTER 11

$\mathcal{M}$ ay we go to the park today, Miss Elliot?" the boys asked as soon as she stepped into the nursery to greet them.

"Maybe." She walked over to look out of the window. "It is very windy. It even looks as though it might rain."

"What is this?" Mr. Fielding asked as he entered the nursery behind her. Adelaide looked up in surprise. She had come to say good morning to the boys and tell them that she planned to leave. Then she had realized the boys' tutors were enjoying a day's reprieve, and Freddy and Harry wished her to partake in some activity with them.

"We wish to go to the park, sir. I will not chase the ducks into the lake," Harry promised.

"I think there is going to be a storm," Adelaide said.

Mr. Fielding walked to the window and looked up at the sky. He then opened the window and held his hand out. "Before a storm is the best time to fly a kite."

Adelaide's heart gave a squeeze. Could the odious man stop being so charming? She firmed her resolve to leave. The longer she stayed near him the worse it would be later. "There you are, boys. Mr.

Fielding has volunteered to fly kites with you in the park," she said, casting him a devilish grin.

He returned her glance with equal deviousness. "And Miss Elliot wishes to join us! I believe Percy knows where it is stored if you care to go and ask him."

She should have anticipated that. The boys gave shouts of pleasure and scuttled off to find the kite.

She was left standing alone with Mr. Fielding, and he was watching her in a way that made her want to squirm, but she held on to her composure.

"That was very sly of you," he remarked.

"I beg your pardon, sir. Did you not intend to join them at the park? I thought you knew it was the tutors' day off."

"I did, in fact, but I enjoy setting your back up, if you will excuse a vulgar expression."

Adelaide ignored his comment. "I am glad you are here. I need to talk to you."

"Then you better do so before the stampede begins," he suggested.

"Indeed. I think it would be best if I remove to my friend's house now that they are in Town."

For a moment, he looked at her, his gaze hooded as it so often was. "I see. Are you unhappy here?"

"No, sir, quite the opposite, in fact." She could not lie. "However, I assumed the situation with your aunt would be temporary and that she would soon wish to return to her own home. I cannot impose further upon so little reason as the desire to vex my aunt."

"Where do you wish to be?" He continued to watch her very closely, and she could feel her cheeks warming. She could not answer that truthfully, for that way lay heartbreak.

She was saved from answering by two sets of feet running back up the stairs to the nursery. "We found it!" Freddy walked in, carrying a red and white kite almost as tall as he was.

"Excellent. We will meet you downstairs in ten minutes. Miss Elliot?"

Adelaide frowned. "I fear I will have to forgo the adventure in the park today, boys." She knelt down to their level. "Now that you have tutors, there is no good reason for me to stay here. My friends have arrived in Town, and I should stay with them now."

Harry's chin began to quiver and Freddy glared at her with anger.

"What did we do wrong this time? I thought we had been good!" Harry cried.

"You have been good, my dears. It is not proper for me to stay here now, since I am no longer your governess."

"Why can't you be our mother?" the little boy asked, full of innocence. "I do not remember my mother, but I should very much like you to be our mama now."

Adelaide pulled him into her arms and tried not to cry. "Oh, Harry, I will still visit you often, I promise."

"You are leaving like everyone else does. It's not fair!" Freddy exclaimed and he slammed the kite down before running down the stairs.

Adelaide felt as though she had been knifed directly in the chest. She had grown very attached to the boys, especially since they were behaving better, and it was hard for her to leave them. From a child's point of view, it must look as though she did not want to be with them.

"Should we go after him?" She looked up at Fielding.

"I will go and see where he is, but he might need a little time to let his temper cool." A loud crack of thunder sounded, rattling the windows, and Harry held onto her with all his might.

"I suspect he will not have gone too far," Mr. Fielding said before he left the nursery.

The rain and wind began to beat against the windows, and Adelaide hoped the boy was merely sulking in a dry, warm corner of the house. Guilt began to assail her...yet how could she have known how the boy would react?

"Should we go and discover where Freddy is?" Adelaide asked Harry.

"He runs away when he gets cross," the boy remarked around the thumb he had decided to place in his mouth.

"Harry, big boys do not suck their thumbs," Adelaide scolded with a suggestion of normalcy. The boy quickly pulled it out of his mouth and stuck it behind his back.

They descended the stairs to the entrance hall, where Mr. Fielding was giving orders to four male servants.

"What has happened?" Adelaide asked as she watched the footmen and Mr. Fielding donning coats and hats.

"Freddy ran out of the front door."

"Into this weather?" she asked, not expecting a reply.

"Percy chased after him, but he is too old to keep up with a ten-year-old boy."

"Where do you think he could have gone? He does not know his way around the city. There are so many dangers out there!" She walked up and down the hall as she fretted.

"I am guessing he will go somewhere familiar. The park is the only place they have gone regularly. Am I right, Harry?"

The boy was sucking his thumb again, but he nodded.

"I will come with you," Adelaide said and at once hurried towards the stairs to change into her sturdy boots.

"You stay here with Harry. I think you have done quite enough for today," he snapped as he hastened out of the door.

Adelaide retreated as though she had been slapped. It was exactly the reminder she needed of the darker side to Mr. Fielding's character, but she would not sit by idly while Freddy was out there in a storm. By this time, Mrs. Percy and some of the maids had come to see what the fuss was about. Adelaide explained and left Harry in their care, asking them to prepare warm food and clothing for everyone's return. She went to don her coat and boots before also heading out into the storm.

Trying to imagine where an angry, scared boy would go to hide, she walked towards the park, shielding her face from the cold, driving rain. It never failed to amaze her how England's weather could change seasons in the blink of an eye.

All the horrors which could happen to a small child in a strange city, irrespective of the foul weather, began to occupy her mind. Fortunately, before she panicked, she realized such foolhardy conjecturing would soon render her worthless in the search for him. Resolving not to think on anything but where he might be, she examined every possible hiding place between the house and the park. It was six streets away, and fortunately there was little traffic about, with the rain beating sideways. Her skirts and stockings were soaked within minutes, and her face was already numbing with chills. She searched every door and alley on her way to the park, but reached it without any sight of the young boy. Remembering occasions when Philip had been upset as a boy, she recalled he had run and run until he was out of breath. Perhaps Freddy in his anger had run without stopping until he reached the park? As she crossed the street and went through the gates, she saw some of Fielding's servants hunting for the boy. Adelaide looked around her, thinking of all the many places to hide in the vast park, and tried not to become disheartened. Beyond the open area dotted with trees, there was the old gravel pit which took overflow water from the Serpentine, an earth embankment with cascade and a dark, forbidding wood. Then there was the Serpentine itself… She swallowed hard. Instead of easing, the storm had intensified, with streaks of lightning and loud roars of thunder shaking the earth.

Anybody's natural inclination would be to seek shelter, so Adelaide decided to go first to the nearest places she could remember. Since the servants appeared to be making a thorough search of every bush and tree, she hastened towards the bridge near the Serpentine. Beneath the bridge there was a sluice to take the excess water to the lower lake. There might be sufficient room near the bank for a small boy to hide. When she reached the spot, however, Freddy was nowhere to be seen. Adelaide stared out over the low railing. The filthy waters lapped at the arches of the little bridge, spelling probable death to any who fell in. She looked wildly about her. Surely, there would be some sign of him, were he in the river? The whole area was empty; sensible folk had taken shelter. Where else might he go? Hidden among a thicket of tall trees beside the carriage road to the north of the Serpentine, there was a refreshment house. She hesitated to go there unattended, but although the landlord looked at her askance, he had not seen Freddy. Neither was the boy to be found at the Guard House or the Cock Pit.

Adelaide was beginning to feel unnerved. She dared not go too far from the carriage road, since much of the park was wild and lonely. Neither did she know how much time had passed, but she could no longer feel her fingers or her toes. Hopefully, Freddy had come to his senses and returned to the house, but would Mr. Fielding not have sent someone to tell her so, if that were the case? Wiggling her toes and rubbing her hands together to try and recover some sensation, she continued searching. If only she had remembered to break her fast that morning, she chastised herself, and if only the park were not so big. They could search for days and never find him, she realized, becoming more disheartened than she already was as she continued to put one foot in front of the other. Nevertheless, she was determined not to give up, so this boy would know how much she cared.

WHY OH WHY is this happening to me? Robert thought begrudgingly as he walked out into the storm. It only wanted this for the whole episode to be a complete farce. He would be the brunt of his friends' jokes for years, if they ever caught wind of what two children had reduced him to. He was tempted to let the boy be cold for a while, for Robert had done this very thing as a boy—at about the age of Freddy—when his own father had died. His moods had become erratic at times and he had needed reassurance. Were Freddy not alone in a strange, big city, Robert would leave him until he had calmed down. But the boy could be in danger—the Lord knew they were good at finding it—and any kind of tragedy could befall him.

Robert had to admit he had not understood the depth of attachment the boys had formed with Miss Elliot. He himself had fallen victim to her charms, so he should not be surprised. He had been too harsh with her and would have to apologize later. In addition, he was rather angry about her announcement to leave, but he could not make her stay. The thought of her remaining and being a mother to the boys was not an unpleasant thought, but she clearly did not wish for them to be a family or she would not be asking to leave.

Robert's mood souring further, he angrily slashed through the bushes around the Serpentine with his cane. Being a parent was a wretched business, he reflected. He found he did care what happened to the boys. They had wormed their way into his hardened heart, apparently. He had even been looking forward to flying the kite with them, of all things!

The storm intensified and brought with it a chilling wind. If they did not find Freddy soon, he would suffer from the elements. Robert pondered returning to the house for more servants to hunt, but he hated to lose any time. He and his men had searched thoroughly around the entire Serpentine, and was satisfied the boy was not there. He stopped under the trees on the embankment to collect his thoughts. Where the deuce had the boy gone?

When his own father had died, he had wanted to be as close to him as possible. The only thing Robert had found comfort in was horses. Perhaps the boy had not run off to the park, but to the mews, where his pony was.

Robert turned immediately and headed back to the house. When he reached the long building where the horses were stabled, he found his suspicions were correct. Freddy was sitting in the stall, huddled up with his pony.

The boy looked up at him, his eyes red and his face swollen from crying. Robert said nothing but entered the stall and slid down next to him.

The pony nickered and thrust his nose into Robert's face. He stroked the roan's muzzle and waited for Freddy to speak. It took a while.

"We have been searching in the park for you, in the storm. We were very worried about you."

Freddy glanced at him as though this surprised him.

"Do you know, my father died when I was about your age. I used to be very, very angry and run away sometimes—but, I always came back."

"You did?"

"I realized I had nowhere better to go. I would have missed my horse very badly, and I knew my aunt and uncle cared for me. Even if they were not my parents, it was not a bad place to be."

Freddy hung his head. "It is not fair!"

"No it is not. We are not promised that life will be fair. However, you still have much to be grateful for. I care about you, and Miss Elliot cares about you."

"Then why is she leaving us? Everybody I love leaves me."

"Your parents did not choose to die, Freddy."

"Miss Elliot is not dead!" he argued.

"No," Robert answered carefully. "She is in a difficult situation herself. Her parents have died and her brother is missing from the army. She must make her own way and she feels as though she is not needed here any more."

"Then you must make her stay!"

"I appreciate your confidence in me," he said dryly. "I will do my best, but if she does not choose to stay, we will resolve how to go on together. You must be brave for Harry, too."

"Promise me?"

"I promise."

"Now, let us go back inside where it is warm and dry. If my guess is right, Cook will have warm biscuits waiting."

When they went into the house, they entered through the kitchens and Robert delivered Freddy into the capable hands of Cook, who immediately began to cuddle him and ply him with warm chocolate and biscuits.

Robert sent a lackey to call off the searchers, then went to change out of his drenched clothing. He passed Miss Elliot's bedchamber and paused to knock. He had expected to see her downstairs with Harry, but when he knocked on her door, she did not answer. He ran back down the stairs.

"Percy, where is Miss Elliot?"

"Why, she left straight after you, sir, to search for Master Freddy. Did she not return with you?"

Robert wanted to scream and bellow to the heavens. Instead, he put his sodden hat and coat back on and downed a shot of brandy to warm his insides. The rain still continued to pour down, but the thunder and lightning had ceased. He set out on foot, then turned back to the stables. It would be much faster to find her on horseback, since she was not hiding. Once mounted on a tall covert hack, he set straight for the park hoping against hope that it would be simple to find her.

"Small favours," he muttered cynically.

On reaching the park again, he passed the servants who had been out searching. Miss Elliot was not with them. "Have any of you seen Miss Elliot?"

"I saw her when we first began searching, sir. She headed towards the bridge near the water."

"Have none of you seen her since?"

The four drenched men shook their heads. "Go back to the house and warm yourselves. Tell Percy to give you each some of my finest brandy."

"Thank you, sir," the men said appreciatively, hurrying off.

Robert had been near the bridge himself, and she had not been there before. Miss Elliot was not a child, and surely she knew her limits, but he still felt anxious for her, having been out in the weather so long. It had been several hours since they first set out, and it was now late afternoon. He should return to the house and wait for her, but he could not bring himself to do it.

If he had known she had intended to go out, he would have asked her to stay within sight of the other hunters, as he had done the servants. If he had kept his cursed mouth shut, instead of venting his anger at her, she might have stayed in the house. Thankfully, the army had trained him well for this, or he would be tempted to panic.

Robert took the same path he had taken before on the footpath along Rotten Row until he saw the water, then veered onto the path towards the bridge. If he had not glanced twice, he would have missed her, for she was sitting in the tunnel beside the bridge, at the nearest arch's edge. Hunched over, even from the footpath he could see she was shivering.

CHAPTER 12

*a*delaide!" Mr. Fielding shouted her name as he came towards her—was she imagining him?

"S-s-so c-c-cold. Just w-w-warming up a bit, sir." She tried to smile at him through her chattering teeth.

"Good God, woman!" Mr. Fielding pulled her to her feet, and throwing off his greatcoat, swiftly wrapped it around her. He ran his hands up and down her arms to warm them. "You are half frozen! We must get you home at once!"

"Freddy?" she asked, hoping the word would portray her question. It was too much effort to speak in full sentences. It felt so very nice to be in his arms, but she dared not say so. If only her clothes were not dripping wet, she might be able to enjoy the sensation more.

"Master Freddy," he said severely, "is safely at home in front of the fire, being coddled by Cook and Mrs. Percy." He was looking at her in that way again, and warmth began to creep into her bones.

"Why do you look at me like that?" she asked before thinking better of it. Her mind was foggy and she might well regret it later, but it was too late for concern now; the words could not be retracted.

"Because I cannot seem to help myself."

He cradled her face in his hands, and she felt her brow wrinkle. "I do not understand," she whispered.

"Neither do I," he said, and his lips descended to hers.

Adelaide had always wondered what it would be like to be kissed, but she was too shocked that he, of all men, was the first one! It made no sense. Feeling was beginning to return, in the form of thousands of tiny pin-pricks all over her body, and a strange sensation also began to spread from her insides outward.

"Kiss me back, Adelaide," he said against her lips.

"I thought I was," she murmured.

He laughed. "You mean to tell me you cannot feel my kissing you? I am undone!"

"Well, I feel a little. Perhaps you should try again," she suggested.

"Minx," he chastised without heat. "I will make certain you feel it, then." Bending forward to oblige her, he pressed harder this time and even nipped at her lower lip. She gasped against his firm mouth; such possibilities had never occurred during late night discussions with her friends. "I will make certain you feel it."

He continued a gentle exploration of her lips, and as a growing warmth chased the chills away, she began to think his methods excellent. He cradled her to him and slanted his head over hers. Their lips met and she was carried to dizzying heights of passion. As she thawed, she bravely attempted to kiss him back and was pleased when she heard him groan with pleasure and look down at her with a devastating smile.

"Come. Much though I would enjoy kissing you more, I am being selfish. You need a hot meal and to be thawed in front of a fire." Before she knew what he was about, he picked her up and began carrying her towards his horse, which was grazing on the wet grass near the banks. The horse did not seem to mind as she was helped onto its back, and Mr. Fielding mounted behind her.

Although he wrapped his arms around her, it was not as warm as the tunnel had been, for the rain was now pelting into her face. Fortunately, the ride to the house took only a few minutes. Dismounting at the front entrance, Mr. Fielding threw the reins to a footman and carried her inside, barking orders as he went. Her maid came running, and very soon, after a hot bath, Adelaide was sitting before a roaring fire, snugly wrapped in dry clothing and blankets, and sipping steaming tea.

~

ONCE ROBERT HAD SEEN Adelaide comfortably ensconced in a deep armchair, the bluish tinge fading from her cheeks, he had hurried upstairs to reassure the boys of her safety. He had then retreated to his study to think. There was little question in his mind of the next step he needed to take, but he was not certain Adelaide would agree. She had been responsive to his kiss, despite being near frozen to death—he chuckled at the recollection—but did it mean she would welcome being his wife? Somehow he would have to convince her.

As an innocent, she doubtless did not realize, but the compatibility they shared was rare. Not only was it a physical attraction; it was far more than that—he actually liked her. There were few females he could spar with as an equal, and he did not think he would ever grow bored. If he did, would he really be any worse case? Besides Harry and Freddy, they would soon set up their own nursery, and he was rather enchanted by the thought of blond boys, and girls with black curls and blue eyes, running about Harlton Park...once it was repaired from the fire, he thought dryly.

A knock on the door disturbed his musings, and Aunt Phillyda's face peeped around the polished panel.

"May I join you?"

"Of course," he said, rising. "May I pour you a drink?"

She considered his amber liquid. "I'll take some of that," she answered, with a naughty twinkle in her eye.

He poured her some brandy, and sat in the chair flanking the fire next to her.

"What happened today?" she asked.

"Freddy ran away."

"That much I gathered. What made him do such a thing?"

"Miss Elliot announced she was leaving to stay with her friends."

"Hmm. I wondered if that was the case. I think they fancy the notion of her being their new mother."

"You think correctly. Harry said as much."

"I have just come from Adelaide's bedchamber," she remarked casually.

"Is she well?" He cast a sideways glance at his aunt.

"She was a little distraught, to be frank, which is surprising for one who has been rescued and is now warm and dry. She should be sound asleep."

"What is the matter?" he asked, sitting up straight. He could not abide prevarication.

"I think you had better ask her."

Looking at his aunt with suspicion, he saw that her face was a mask of bland innocence. It was not as though he did not intend to make Adelaide his wife, but he would brook no manipulation from anyone in their courtship. "Very well. I shall ascertain if she wishes for my assistance."

Trying not to worry, he still took the steps two at a time. When he reached her door, he leaned his head against it, wondering what he should say to her. No sounds came from within the room, so she was not wearing out the carpet with anxiety. Could she have developed a fever from being out in the elements so long? He lifted a hand and knocked lightly on the door.

"Yes?" she questioned softly.

He opened the door and found her sitting before the fire, her knees bent and tucked beneath her thick cotton night-rail. She sat very still and watched him warily. "You should not be in here."

"No, probably I should not," he conceded. "I will leave the door open, that being the case, but my aunt seemed to think I should speak with you. Is something amiss? Have you warmed sufficiently?"

"Yes. My hands and feet are no longer blue, thank you. Your servants are very attentive."

"Then what has my aunt so concerned? Are you still considering leaving?"

"Lady Middleton should not have said anything to you." She fixed her eyes on the fire, appearing entranced.

"She did not betray your confidence. Her concern is genuine," he pleaded gently, with a softness he was unaccustomed to. Why would she not speak to him?

Adelaide turned her gaze from the fire and finally looked at him. There was no anger, no mischief, but genuine pain. He walked closer to her and sank down on his knees across from her. She continued to watch him.

He reached out his hand and gently wiped away a tear which was escaping down her cheek. He did not trouble to disguise the hunger he was sure must be in his eyes. Carefully, he captured her hands in his; he needed to see for himself that she was warm.

"I cannot do this," she whispered.

"Do what?" he asked, though he knew what she was thinking. He wanted to hear her say it.

"Be your, your…" She obviously could not bring herself to say it, the silly chit.

"Mistress?" he supplied.

She frowned at him and gave him a reluctant nod.

"That is not what I was offering, my dear."

Her cheeks reddened and her eyes flashed, an excellent sign, he thought with some satisfaction.

"Then I shall be on my way, first thing in the morning," she retorted.

"As you wish, my dear, but I was rather hoping you would stay and be my wife," he added imperturbably.

It was pure delight to watch the emotions cross Adelaide's face. It was apparent she had had no suspicion of either his next words, or yet his intent.

"I do not know what to say," she answered, still looking stunned.

"You could say you would be honoured to be my wife…or you could tell me to go to the devil."

A wry look of mischief crossed her face. "However tempting, I do not think I wish you to the devil, even though you are insufferable at times."

"And at other times?"

"Other times I find you perplexing."

"Do, pray, continue." He rubbed his thumb over her hand and noticed her breathing quicken, as he himself was drawn to her soft scent of roses and soap from her bath.

"I find myself attracted to you," she admitted shyly, "but I have never dreamed you might offer for me. I...why me? The whole of England knows you vowed never to marry."

"You enchant me." He shrugged a shoulder in a careless fashion. "I enjoy being with you. I found myself jealous for the first time even though I knew James was doing it deliberately."

"You knew?"

"Of course. He would never make himself so ridiculous over a lady if not for good purpose."

She laughed and the sound warmed his heart. "I cannot imagine you being jealous of anything."

"I found it quite shocking as well. Does this mean you will say yes?"

"You have not asked only because of the boys, have you? I think they will be happy enough once they go to school."

"I can say with certainty it is because of the boys. Without them, I would not have found you. Without them, you would not have scared me to death today. I suspected from the first moment I saw you covered in soot that you would tempt me, but it took a while for me to convince myself it was the right thing for both of us. Will you be mine, sweet Adelaide?"

"I still cannot believe you want me." She shook her head, as if to wake herself up.

"What will it take to convince you?" He leaned forward and kissed her forehead lightly, then peppered kisses on her cheeks, her eyes, her ears, until he elicited a giggle.

"That feels lovely," she whispered.

He teased her lips with his and she melted against him. She kissed him back eagerly, hinting at the hidden passion he knew lay beneath the cloak of propriety. "You had better answer me, my love. I suspect Aunt Phyllida will soon arrive to force your hand. I want the choice to be yours completely."

"Yes," she murmured against his lips with a smile. "This is the last thing I expected."

"I expect our future to be full of surprises," he mused.

"I find the thought no longer bothers me so much. For now, though, sir, I want you to hush and kiss me again."

"As you wish, my love."

.

EPILOGUE

*E*veryone was delighted with the news that Adelaide and Robert were to be married—especially Harry and Freddy. Adelaide wanted a small ceremony, with only their closest friends in attendance, since Philip was still missing and the rest of her family was gone. She did not count Lady Hogg, of course. Her aunt's standing in Society had suffered immeasurably once the *ton* had discovered the dreadful way she had treated Adelaide.

With Waverley's goodwill, the happy couple chose to marry at Somerton, in the small chapel coloured with stain glass inside to match the beauty outside. Adelaide dressed in a pale green silk gown, and clasped the simple pearls she had worn all Season about her neck and in her ears. Robert had gifted her with an oval-shaped sapphire ring to grace her hand and as she walked from the house, she could not believe she was marrying him. Nevertheless, she could not help but shed a few tears when the Duke of Waverley took her arm to escort her forward to the altar, for she felt so guilty knowing such happiness whilst Philip was missing.

"He wants you to be happy," the Duke leaned over to whisper in her ear.

She nodded. "I know, but it is still hard not to wish he were here."

"He wants to be here, I assure you. By the way, Tobin has arrived and would like to speak with you after the ceremony."

"He is?" She stretched her neck back and looked at him with surprise.

"Yes, but do not think on it now. Enjoy your moment."

They walked along the small aisle, where their friends and families were sitting in the pews. The vows were short and sweet without the formality of a Society wedding, yet she felt the sincerity of Robert's commitment to her in her heart, for his gaze seared into hers with each word. After they had both said, 'I will,' Freddy and Harry, who had been behaving admirably, whooped with pleasure.

The wedding breakfast was held in the gardens overlooking the Thames. Somerton was at its best in the height of summer with bright pink roses set off by the violet-blue hydrangea bushes nearby.

An array of pastries, fruits, cheeses and breads had been arranged on the terrace, and after the ceremony, Adelaide walked beside Robert to partake of this sumptuous feast. Now they could relax and enjoy themselves in the informal atmosphere, with only friends surrounding them.

"Are you sure you wish to go to France, Mrs. Fielding?" her husband asked as he served her a piece of delectable-looking cake.

"I realize it is the last place you wish to go, but my heart will not be easy until I have searched for Philip myself."

"As you wish, my dearest," he replied agreeably. Reaching over, he licked a piece of icing from her lip and then kissed her cheek.

"Can ye not save the *phógadh* for later?" a dark-haired man dressed in Regimentals demanded in a deep, Irish brogue.

"Tobin," Robert drawled. "I almost missed your insolence."

Tobin grinned and Adelaide was quite certain the man must leave hearts breaking in a devastating swath behind him wherever he went. He turned his gaze upon her. "Wheesht! As I live and breathe, Philip looks much bonnier as a lass."

"Thank you, Tobin. I am Adelaide...Mrs. Fielding." She held out her hand and Tobin lingered over it, drawing a scowl from Robert.

"The Duke said you wish to speak with me. About Philip, I presume? Please say you have good news."

Tobin drew them both aside, away from the music and laughter of the wedding celebration.

"We received a letter from your brother, in code."

"So he is alive!" Adelaide exclaimed with relief. She clutched her husband's arm with joy.

"Yes, it appears so. However, the message asked us to stop searching for him, as best we can decipher it."

"I do not understand." Adelaide frowned.

"Perhaps he is on a secret mission, my love. He will tell us more when he is able, I am sure. For now, let it be enough to know he is alive," Robert reassured her. Thanking Tobin, he pulled Adelaide into an impromptu waltz, drawing cheers from the small crowd.

"Stop frowning or people will think you are a reluctant bride."

"Do not be ridiculous. My mind is worrying over Philip, that is all."

"Your mind should be relieved of all care, not worried," he insisted.

"I am relieved, but I would feel better could I see him, safe at home, with my own eyes."

"I think you will see him before long. With Napoleon exiled, Philip should be able to find his way home to you soon. Now, Mrs. Fielding, I insist you redirect your thoughts to your new husband."

She looked up into his tawny eyes, which held the perfect mix of love and devilry. "Oh, I think the boys might need me," she prevaricated with equal mischief.

"The boys are quite capable of amusing themselves, and they are not our problem for the next few weeks," he riposted.

She cast a look of doubt at him. At that very moment, Freddy and Harry were wading through the ornamental fountain in the garden, to fish out a ball. "Very well then, my dear sir, I resolve to think of only you for the entirety of our wedding trip."

"That is more like it," he said amiably, dropping a chaste kiss on her nose. "I have never thought you suited to being a governess, anyway."

PREVIEW THE HEIRESS

BY LAURA BEERS

*N*icholas watched his ward turn around, and he saw a flicker of fear in her eyes. Good. She should be afraid of him. But to his astonishment, it was quickly replaced with determination. He had not expected that.

He had another problem. Penelope was not the young miss that he had envisioned. She was a beautiful woman with brown hair, slim nose, elegant cheekbones, and wide, expressive blue eyes that would enchant even the weakest fool.

His first responsibility was to ensure that his ward knew her place and understood that he was in charge. "Explain to me why I should not cane you for your deliberate attempt to deceive me?" he asked.

"You would not dare," she replied defiantly.

He took a commanding step towards her. "It is within my rights as your guardian."

"My intention was for you to allow me to stay at Brighton Hall by appearing unmarriageable," she explained in a rational tone.

"For what purpose?" he asked, his voice strained.

Rather than cower, or step back, his ward tilted her head to look up at him. "I refuse to go to London and be married off without so much as a say in my life."

"You are an heiress. It would be in your best interest to marry, and quickly."

"I have no intention of marrying this Season," she asserted.

That would not do. If Miss Foster didn't marry this Season, then she would remain his ward for another year. Another burden. "Regardless, you will go to London for the Season, and my mother will introduce you into society," he said, his tone brooking no argument. Once she got to London, he was positive that she would see reason.

"I will not," came her quick reply.

His eyes narrowed at her impertinence. He had just issued an order. "It was not a request," he grunted.

"I perceived as much."

Insubordination. "You are not in a position to deny my request."

To his surprise, she drew herself up to her full height before saying, "I know exactly what you intend to do with me, your grace," she said in a matter-of-fact tone. "Your plan is to marry me off at your first opportunity, because I am only a burden to you."

Nicholas had to admit that she was a clever, determined thing. However, these were not good qualities for a woman to possess if she ever hoped to marry. "I am not so callous as to marry you off without first discussing it with you."

She arched a perfectly shaped eyebrow. "Why should you, a man that I have never met before now, have control over my future? How is that fair?"

"It's not, but you are a woman," he contended, "and as such, you need the protection of a man."

"Then I will hire guards to ensure my safety."

"That will not be sufficient." Nicholas glared down at her, but she met his gaze with a fiery intensity. This would not do. He couldn't very well beat the girl into submission. He needed to change tactics. It was time to negotiate. He took a step back and pointed towards the sofa. "Perhaps if we can come to a new understanding."

Penelope eyed him suspiciously. "What do you propose?"

Your surrender.

ELIZABETH JOHNS

. . .

PURCHASE The Heiress Now

AFTERWORD

Author's note: British spellings and grammar have been used in an effort to reflect what would have been done in the time period in which the novels are set. While I realize all words may not be exact, I hope you can appreciate the differences and effort made to be historically accurate while attempting to retain readability for the modern audience.

Thank you for reading *The Governess*. I hope you enjoyed it. If you did, please help other readers find this book:

1. This ebook is lendable, so send it to a friend who you think might like it so she or he can discover me, too.
2. Help other people find this book by writing a review.
3. Sign up for my new releases at www.Elizabethjohnsauthor.com, so you can find out about the next book as soon as it's available.
4. Come like my Facebook page www.facebook.com/Elizabethjohnsauthor or follow on Instagram @Ejohnsauthor or feel free to write me at elizabethjohnsauthor@gmail.com

ACKNOWLEDGMENTS

There are many, many people who have contributed to making my books possible.

My family, who deals with the idiosyncrasies of a writer's life that do not fit into a 9 to 5 work day.

Dad, who reads every single version before and after anyone else— that alone qualifies him for sainthood.

The cover artists, who take my visions and interprets them, making them into works of art people open in the first place.

My team of friends who care about my stories enough to help me shape them before everyone else sees them.

Heather who helps me say what I mean to!

And to the readers who make all of this possible.
I am forever grateful to you all.

ABOUT THE AUTHOR

Like many writers, Elizabeth Johns was first an avid reader, though she was a reluctant convert. It was Jane Austen's clever wit and unique turn of phrase that hooked Johns when she was "forced" to read Pride and Prejudice for a school assignment. She began writing when she ran out of her favourite author's books and decided to try her hand at crafting a Regency romance novel. Her journey into publishing began with the release of Surrender the Past, book one of the Loring-Abbott Series. Johns makes no pretensions to Austen's wit but hopes readers will perhaps laugh and find some enjoyment in her writing.

Johns attributes much of her inspiration to her mother, a retired English teacher. During their last summer together, Johns would sit on the porch swing and read her stories to her mother, who encouraged her to continue writing. Busy with multiple careers, including a professional job in the medical field, author and mother of small children, Johns squeezes in time for reading whenever possible.

ALSO BY ELIZABETH JOHNS

Made in the USA
San Bernardino, CA
05 July 2020